ENTANGLED: THE HOMECOMING

BARBARA BRETTON

Free Spirit Press

Praise for Barbara Bretton

Praise for USA Today best-selling author Barbara Bretton

"Bretton's characters are always real and their conflicts believable."
— *Chicago Sun-Times*

"Soul warming... A powerful relationship drama [for] anyone who enjoys a passionate look inside the hearts and souls of the prime players."
— Midwest Book Review

"[Bretton] excels in her portrayal of the sometimes sweet, sometimes stifling ties of a small community. The town's tight network of loving, eccentric friends and family infuses the tale with a gently comic note that perfectly balances the darker dramas of the romance."
— *Publishers Weekly*

"A tender love story about two people who, when they find something special, will go to any length to keep it."
— Booklist

"Honest, witty... absolutely unforgettable."
— Rendezvous

"A classic adult fairy tale."
— *Affaire de Coeur*

"Dialogue flows easily and characters spring quickly to life."
— *Rocky Mountain News*

Chapter 1

DO YOU BELIEVE IN LOVE?

For the first thirty years of my life, I wasn't sure I did. Don't get me wrong, I was a dyed-in-the-wool romantic who spent her evenings mainlining Chips Ahoy while watching the Hallmark Channel. Happily-ever-after endings seemed to work well enough between the covers of books and in the rom coms I devoured by the hour, but in real life?

That was where you lost me.

I mean, when was the last time a handsome knight in shining armor parked his white charger in your driveway and handed you a two-carat princess cut diamond and the keys to Barbie's Dream House?

[Crickets.]

That's what I thought.

Heroes are definitely in short supply in the real world, which was one of the reasons why I spent most of my free time pretending the real world didn't exist.

When Luke MacKenzie came to town to investigate Sugar Maple's first murder, I didn't intend to fall in love. He was mortal, after all, and I knew first-hand how dangerous a combination magicks and mortals made. My own parents' doomed love story was never far from my mind. Mix magick and mortal together and tragedy was right around the corner.

But here's the thing about love: It doesn't care if you're ready. It doesn't care if you believe it has the shelf life of a ripe banana. Love opens you up to life in a way nothing else does and it doesn't ask permission. From that moment on, your heart belongs to someone else and you wouldn't have it any other way.

And, in my case, it brought my magick to life.

By the way, I'm Chloe Hobbs, the half-human/half-sorceress owner of Sticks & Strings, New England's most popular yarn shop. Knitters and spinners from up and down the East Coast (and some as far away as California and Hawaii) flock to our workshops and turn our sales into the fiber junkie's equivalent of Woodstock. You wouldn't think that would be a problem, but when an entire town is trying to hide a secret in plain sight, things can get a little dicey.

My best friends are a witch, a shifter, and a Norwegian troll. My 100% Homo sapiens husband Luke hangs out with a selkie and a werewolf. A family of Fae run the Sugar Maple Inn, a popular rest stop along the Spirit Trail, and our rarely used funeral parlor is owned by a family of vampires. We've been here since my ancestor Aerynn fled Salem with a group of Others and founded Sugar Maple as a sanctuary where they could live in peace.

Of course, the word "peace" is relative but, despite the problems we were currently dealing with, I was optimistic about the future.

Then again, I'm a new mother and a new bride. Optimism seems to come with the territory.

At least it did until the new magicks came to town.

I was born and raised in Sugar Maple and thought I knew all of our biases and prejudices and idiosyncrasies. However, the intensity of dissent from some surprising sources sent me reeling. For centuries, we had worried about hiding our magick from fearful, judgmental humans bent on banishing our kind from their world. I never thought we would become the bad guys.

Unfortunately, that seemed to be exactly what was happening, right before my eyes.

Two months ago I opened up Sugar Maple to leader Rohesia's clan of Others who were escaping their crumbling dimensional home beyond the mist. I had been so sure that the residents of Sugar Maple would embrace the newcomers that I pretty much presented the move as a done deal.

Not my finest hour.

You probably heard the uproar that exploded at our Town Hall meeting last month when I presented the plan to expand Sugar Maple's population. (To be honest, they probably heard the uproar in space.)

Last week one of Paul Griggs's sons had been charged with harassing a young male member of Rohesia's clan and running him into a ditch near the Toothaker Bridge. Two members of our Monday Night Knit Club almost came to blows over donating used clothing to the newcomers to help them blend in more easily with the rest of us. There was even talk about requiring the newcomers to file paperwork with Luke, our Sugar Maple police chief, detailing how they planned to contribute to Sugar Maple's economy.

That one made me laugh. At this point, the members of Rohesia's clan didn't know what an economy was. They were still working on the wonders of indoor plumbing and electricity. Their magick is more elemental than ours. More violent in many ways. Diplomacy wasn't the first weapon in their arsenal, but it should have been the first weapon in ours.

Have you ever found yourself trapped between a rock and a hard place? That was exactly where I found myself now. I owed everything to my extended Sugar Maple family. They were the ones who had surrounded me with love and support after my parents were killed in a car crash. They were the ones who waited patiently for me to gain my powers and take my rightful place as the next heir to Aerynn.

But I owed something to Rohesia and her clan, as well. My parents had betrothed me to her grandson Gavan when I was six years old, pledging my future to a life of Old World ways, Old World magick. In other words, a marriage based on familial duty instead of love.

A marriage Rohesia had counted on to save her community.

The physical structure of their dimension was crumbling faster than predicted. Suddenly time was of the essence. They needed to make life-or-death decisions that would determine whether their clan would move forward or pierce the veil forever.

After over twenty years of silence, Rohesia sent Gavan to investigate rumors of my pending marriage to Luke and to stop it, if necessary. His mission was clear: he was expected to marry me and join our two factions together, no matter what. In a surprising twist, Gavan had refused to break up the family Luke and I had created. He understood what Luke and Laria meant to me and he found the guts to stand up to Rohesia, who was a powerfully intimidating leader.

Somehow we had made Rohesia see reason. Twenty-first century reason. She could have made my life a living hell but she didn't, and because of that act of compassion (at least that's how I choose to view it), Luke and I were able to exchange vows.

Some of Rohesia's clan had chosen to roll the dice and stay in their ancestral home until the end. Some had chosen to pierce the veil on their own terms, taking control of their destiny in the only way that made sense to them. But the majority had campaigned for a move to the human realm where Sugar Maple was viewed as the ultimate success story.

My ancestor Aerynn had founded Sugar Maple as a refuge for magicks seeking safety from a hostile world. As far as I was concerned, it still was.

It was the second Saturday in October and I was holding a Teach Your Kids to Knit workshop at Sticks & Strings that afternoon. My human cousin Wendy had volunteered to drive over from her home in Maine to help out. I loved her and appreciated the offer but I knew that teaching a group of six-year-olds to handle garter stitch wasn't the real attraction.

Rohesia's grandson Gavan was.

"The guy's good," my BFF Janice said as we watched the two of them gazing into each other's eyes over a display of Koigu before the knitters and their children arrived. "He must have attached some kind of GPS gadget to her butt. The second she pulled up this morning in that old white minivan of hers, he manifested."

"He doesn't know from GPS yet," I reminded her. "You're looking at primal attraction, Fae style."

You could feel his intensity across the room.

Janice sighed deeply. "He's a hottie," she said. "I'll give him that."

I nodded. Why debate the obvious?

"She knows it will never work, doesn't she?" Janice asked.

"I've told her what I can about the Fae, but I'm not sure she heard me."

"She doesn't want to hear you," Janice said. "She's in lust."

"She thinks she's in love."

"Women always think it's love but, trust me: first it's lust."

I couldn't argue that point either. For Luke and me, those first days had been all sparks and fireworks like the Fourth of July.

"I even used the Prince Charles analogy," I said. "He might have loved Camilla, but first he had to marry Diana."

"So he could sire an heir and a spare."

"Exactly." And we both knew that imperative was non-negotiable. I lowered my voice. "Wendy can't have children," I said, my eyes misting over as I watched the two lovers pretend they were nothing more than friends. "Even if she had magick, that would be a deal-breaker for him."

The weight of his clan's future rested on his shoulders. Rohesia and her band of Others were still reeling from his decision to break our betrothal bonds, and I knew that the pressure on him to join with a magick from Sugar Maple grew more intense with every day that passed.

Casting in his lot with a mortal who could never bear his child was definitely off the table. Unfortunately, everyone seemed to know that but Gavan and my cousin Wendy.

Janice blew out a long sigh that made me laugh out loud. "I'm no fan of his clan, but I think he might be worth a broken heart."

"I hope so," I said, "because that's the only way it can end."

"Ouch!" My BFF shot me a look. "Cynical much?"

"Just being realistic. She's a twenty-first century human. He's a magick, following rules set in place during a different millennium. I'm not sure even love can bridge that gap."

There was a long, uncomfortable silence, and then Janice said, "You realize it's all your fault."

The words tore through me like buckshot. "What?"

"I know you heard me, Chloe. I said, this whole thing is your fault."

"You're joking, right?"

She shook her head. "Not this time."

I faced her head-on. "You want to be more specific?"

She waved in the general direction of the two prospective lovers. "Him. His cohorts. That Rohesia woman. You never should have opened up Sugar Maple to them."

"Okay," I said, relaxing. "Now I know you're kidding." Janice was a fair, open-minded, compassionate woman whose own fore-mothers had fled persecution in Salem centuries ago for the safety of Sugar Maple.

"I'm not the only one who feels this way. You were at the last Town Hall meeting. You heard what we had to say."

"'We'?" I asked, unable to keep the edge from my voice. "Are you telling me, you're on the side of those--"

"Citizens," Janice supplied. "Townspeople. Life-long residents."

"Okay," I said, aware of the rising tide of my temper. "*Residents.* I can't believe you're coming down on the side of Midge Stallworth and Verna Griggs and the rest of their short-sighted pals."

"Hello," Janice snapped. "Were you at the same meeting I was? Don't lump me in with Midge and Verna, thank you very much. The dissent was widespread and diverse and grounded in reality."

"Is that your Harvard education talking?" I had a temper, but I was rarely bitchy. I wished I could pull back my remark, but it was out there and, unfortunately, it packed a punch.

"That's my common sense talking," she said, flashing a look of disgust my way. "Something you seem to have misplaced. I can't believe Luke didn't rein you in."

"Rein me in?" My voice went high and tight. "He's my husband, not my keeper."

"He's the chief of police," my best friend threw back at me. "I can't believe he wants to open up our town to a group of strangers."

"They're not strangers," I protested. "They were part of the original clan that began in Wales."

"I don't care if we all came here on the same spaceship from Mars," Janice said. "They're strangers to us and to our ways and it's going to get a lot worse around here before it gets better. You had no right to grant them asylum without taking the town's pulse first."

"That's why I called a Town Hall meeting."

"After the fact."

"It's not like I had a choice, Janice. They stopped my wedding. They put all of you into a state of suspended animation. I did what I had to do, when I had to do it."

"Take a look around you, Chloe. My youngest came home with a bloody nose last week and it wasn't because he tripped during gym."

I wanted to remind her that her youngest child came home with a bloody nose at least every other week but I somehow kept my trap shut. "I'm sorry Liam was hurt," I said, meaning it. "Is he okay now?"

She waved a dismissive hand in my general direction. "What is wrong with you?" she exploded. "Don't you get it? Some of the newcomers jumped him on his way home from school and beat him up."

"I don't believe it."

The look she gave me was one of utter disgust. "Somehow I'm not surprised. That entire group has you bought and paid for. How do you explain the broken shop windows? The punctured tires up and down Osborne Street? The kids who mixed it up in the woods over that stupid cave?" She paused for breath. "They weren't fighting themselves, Chloe. They were jumped by some of Rohesia's group."

She made it sound like we were doing a *West Side Story* revival. In another minute, the Jets and the Sharks would be ready for a rumble over a cave where kids made out.

"Sugar Maple isn't perfect," I said as the truth of her words smacked me in the head. "We're not pacifists. We've had problems like this before and worked it all out."

"What's happened to you?" she demanded. "Midge was right. You've changed and not for the better. The old Chloe would have taken everyone into consideration."

"Is that who put you up to this?" My control was shot to hell. "I never thought you'd lower yourself to doing Midge's dirty work for her."

"Open your eyes, girlfriend." Janice's anger clearly matched my own. "Midge is only one of many." She began to enumerate them on her fingers. "Midge. Lynette—"

"Lynette?" My voice was up in dogs-only register. "Why didn't she say something?" Lynette was my other BFF. "I thought we told each other everything."

Janice ignored me. "Lynette," she continued. "Archie. Paul. Lorcan. The crew at Fully Caffeinated. Most of the folks at Assisted Living." She paused. "Want me to go on?"

Suddenly I became aware that Wendy and Gavan had fallen silent and were taking in every harsh and ugly word.

I met Janice's eyes. "I think we've both said enough for now."

"We haven't said near enough." She aimed her gaze at Wendy and Gavan. "Does either one of you know what you're doing to this town?"

They both looked completely bewildered. My heart went out to them.

"Come on, Janice," I said, in as conciliatory a tone as I could manage. "Leave them alone."

"No," she said, without missing a beat. "They're part of the reason we have trouble." She aimed her words directly at the two erstwhile lovers. "It's never going to work. I know it. Chloe knows it.

I'll even bet you two know it. They'll never accept you, Wendy. You don't belong and you never will."

"Janice," I said, my conciliatory tone rapidly hardening. "That's my cousin you're talking to."

"Go on," Janice challenged me. "Tell your cousin how you really feel about the two of them getting together. Tell her what you told me."

Poor Wendy looked as if she had been kicked in the stomach. "Chloe?" Her voice was soft, hesitant.

"I already have," I said. "Wendy knows the situation. Magicks and mortals have a long and unhappy history."

"You should understand," Janice said, switching her attention to Gavan. "You grew up with that history. You know it can't work. There's nothing here for you or any of your friends."

He met her gaze. I had to hand it to him. He didn't so much as blink.

Janice, to my surprise, did.

She grabbed for her tote bag with the Cut & Curl logo emblazoned across the front in bright red letters. "Gotta run," she said, her voice cool and collected. "Coffee break's over."

She waved a quick goodbye to a shell-shocked Wendy and Gavan, kissed Laria on the top of her head, and then darted out the door.

Actually, "shell-shocked" was putting it mildly. The two of them looked like they'd been caught in battlefield crossfire.

"I'm sorry you had to listen to that," I said.

Gavan nodded. "It was not unexpected."

I arched a brow. "You knew she felt that way?"

"Her opinion has been made clear many times."

Apparently Wendy and I were the only ones who were surprised.

"To you?" I asked.

He nodded. "And to Rohesia, among others."

"I can't believe she said those things," Wendy said, the fires of righteous indignation burning brightly. "That's not the Janice I thought I knew."

"It's not the Janice I thought I knew either," I said, struggling with surprise and shock. "She's upset. Her kid got hurt. Maybe we should cut her some slack."

Wendy didn't look like she thought that was a viable option. "You should ask her about--"

Gavan silenced her with a hand on her shoulder. To my surprise, my garrulous cousin fell silent.

Wendy is related to me on my father's side, which means she is mortal, same as Luke. Unfortunately, Gavan is pure Fae. And not just twenty-first century Fae like we know them here in Sugar Maple. Gavan's magick is from another time and place that we were struggling to understand.

But, as I said before, love doesn't always make sense. I guess Luke and I are proof of that. I wouldn't have bet money on a happily-ever-after ending for us when we first met, but here we are, newly married with a baby daughter named Laria. Clearly, almost anything is possible.

Wendy lives in Bailey's Harbor, Maine where she runs a one-woman housecleaning service. Eighteen months ago her husband left her and it didn't help that her ex and his new wife were expecting a baby any day.

This whole thing with Gavan had "rebound" written all over it. Okay, I'll admit my romantic history before I met Luke was pretty much limited to first dates with selkies and shifters. Anything I knew about broken hearts had been learned watching Sex and the City reruns and movies on the Hallmark Channel, but even I understood you had to take things slowly after a broken heart.

Especially when the man in question doesn't play by the same rules you grew up with.

I had tried to explain the seductive power of the Fae to Wendy when I first realized what was happening between them, but she hadn't been listening. Oh, she thought she was. She nodded at the right times and said she agreed with absolutely everything I was saying, but then Gavan would show up in his wildly sexy who-knows-what-century-it's-from clothing and her eyes would glaze over and the two of them would melt into the kind of embrace that sent heat waves racing through your veins just looking at them.

I had grown close to Wendy very quickly, but not so close that I felt I could order her to stay away from him. It was her heart, her life. If he made her happy even for just a little while, then maybe a fling with a Fae would be worth it.

But, no matter how you looked at it, there was an expiration date clearly stamped on their relationship.

To be honest, I wasn't exactly sure how that made me feel.

I glanced at the wall clock and shifted into work mode. Goodie bags were filled and ready. The store fridge was loaded with juice boxes, bottles of water, and an assortment of sliced fruits and veggies. A towering mountain of cookies, wrapped in brightly colored plastic wrap, rested on the credenza. The only thing left to do was make sure we had the project bags ready for the attendees, both big and small.

"Our guests will be arriving soon, Gavan." I almost felt guilty for cutting their romantic morning interlude short but my fight with Janice had already done that for me.

He understood it wouldn't be easy to explain the presence of a gorgeous six foot six inch guy in an embroidered cloak to a store filled with nosy knitters and their offspring.

He said something to Wendy and she nodded.

The look that passed between them could melt gold. He touched her cheek with his hand. She leaned into the touch, eyes closing for a moment.

And then, in the blink of an eye, he was gone.

Wendy had the dazed, glassy-eyed look of a woman in love and it awoke a wild mixture of emotions inside me. I wanted only happiness for her but I knew she would never find it with Gavan.

"You don't have to say anything, Chloe." Her voice was softer than I had ever heard it. "I know."

Did she? She was in love and love did crazy things to a person.

Especially a mortal in love with a Fae.

"Just be careful," I said. "Gavan has a good heart but he already defied Rohesia and the Others once. He can't do that again."

My chatty cousin smiled and didn't say another word about it and, to my credit, neither did I.

~

But that didn't mean I stopped thinking about it.

The confrontation with Janice had left me deeply rattled and I struggled to corral my unruly emotions and concentrate on the workshop. Janice was the sister I never had and the rift between us tore at my heart in a way I had never felt before.

Suddenly I was deeply grateful that the rest of the day would be filled with lots of yarn and dozens of happy knitters.

Knitting was my happy place. Give me a pair of US3s and some sock yarn and my worries vanish in a blur of knits and purls. I loved everything about the process: choosing yarns; deciding on the right needle size; working the finicky first round; even ripping the whole thing out and starting over. And I especially loved spreading the knitting gospel to the next generation of needleworkers.

The workroom was alive with enthusiasm. Shrieks of laughter alternated with stretches of concentration as the kids (and their equally enthusiastic parents) put their new skills to work.

Imagine, if you will, twenty kids under seven years of age and twenty parents over seven years of age, all of them yarned and dangerous. Most of the parents were fairly accomplished knitters (or advanced beginners), but their kids were completely unfamiliar with anything to do with yarn, knitting, or sitting still for longer than fifty-two seconds straight. (And, yes, I timed them.)

My ten-month-old baby girl watched quietly from her car seat next to my chair, her beautiful burnished gold eyes taking in everything. I wondered what was going on in her tiny head. Mostly I found myself praying to the goddesses of magick that her human DNA would carry the day and keep her from stealing the spotlight from the knitting itself. Laria had already displayed an alarming mastery of her powers, powers that far outstripped my own still-new magick, and had been known to act out in a very memorable fashion.

Let's put it this way: my daughter could fly before she could walk.

Just try baby-proofing an entire town.

"Tell me again why you thought a Teach Your Kids to Knit workshop was a good idea," Wendy murmured as she grabbed another skein of Brown Sheep worsted from the dwindling supply.

"Because I'm crazy, that's why," I murmured back, as I scanned the room for signs of anarchy.

"Ethan!" one of the mothers bellowed. "Leave that poor cat alone and finish your row of garter stitch now."

Three Ethans checked to see which one of them was being called out. Two Masons played catch with a ball of Madelinetosh. Penelope, my beloved feline companion, burrowed deeper into the basket of roving she called home and ignored everyone.

Multiple Lilys, Olivias, Liams. A rogue Tiffany, one Marco and more. Mostly they were a blur of giggles and juice boxes to me as their mothers tried desperately to keep them focused on the project at hand. Next time, if there was a next time, I'd cut the number of participants in half and make sure I had plenty of red wine waiting for me at home when it was over.

At least my baby daughter was having fun. A darling little girl named Ava, who sported a hot pink crocheted flower in her hair, had settled herself next to Laria and was earnestly explaining the facts of knitting to her while she worked an amazingly great-looking strip of garter stitch. Laria watched with her usual intensity. I had no way of knowing exactly what she was able to understand but if the topic was magick, we were in trouble.

"Ava loves babies," her mother said, joining me near the mini-fridge. "I hope you don't mind."

"Not at all," I said. "Laria's having a great time."

"I'm Mallory," she said. "I called for directions this morning. I'm the one who got lost on her way here from the Motel 6."

"Chloe," I said with an answering grin. "The one who had to hand the phone over to someone who could actually give you directions."

"I usually rely on my GPS, but it quit on me when I left the highway." She shook her head. "That's what I get for buying used cars."

I didn't tell her that the problem wasn't her GPS but Sugar Maple itself. Instead, we chatted briefly about the squirrely roads outside of town.

"The thing you have to remember," I said, "is that there's only one road in and out of town."

Mallory rolled her eyes. "And every other road leads into the woods."

"Sometimes it seems that way."

She laughed again and her daughter looked up at us, and then turned her attention back to Laria.

"Ava has a lot of patience for such a young child," I said, watching the interaction between our daughters. "Does she have any brothers or sisters?"

"Not yet," Mallory said with a quick smile. "I hope her patience with Laria will translate to a baby brother or sister one day." She met my eyes. "Is Laria your first?"

I nodded. "I still have my training wheels on."

"I remember those days," Mallory said. "I was sure everything I did was going to ruin her life."

"Exactly! She's made it clear she's over nursing and prefers the bottle, but I'm the one who can't let go." My embarrassingly teary outbursts each time she refused the breast testified to that fact.

We watched as Ava deftly turned her work and began knitting a new row.

"I'm a pretty good teacher," I said, "but I don't think I can take credit for Ava's progress today. She knew how to knit before she got here, didn't she?"

"She's watched me knit," Mallory admitted, "but as far as I know, this is the first time she's tried it."

"She's a natural," I said. "I may be taking lessons from her before too long."

Mallory beamed with pleasure. "She's full of surprises," she said. "Just wait until yours gets a little older. You'll see."

I wisely refrained from sharing my flying baby stories. Any more surprises like that and I would be grey before my time.

We chatted for another minute or two. Mallory asked if she could plug in her phone.

"We're heading to Rhode Island to visit my husband's parents and I expect to get lost at least three times along the way."

"Help yourself," I said. "I don't know how the pioneers managed without smartphones."

We shared a laugh at the thought of prairie schooners outfitted with Wi-Fi and GPS, and then I moved on to see how the other workshop attendees were faring. They were all good kids, even if they had the attention spans of gnats. Most of them seemed eager to learn even if only in five minute spurts.

I was pathetically grateful to Wendy for volunteering to help out. Teaching kids to knit might not take a village, but it definitely required more than one instructor, if only to keep the chaos at bay.

Now I understood why Janice and Lynette had laughed themselves into coughing fits when I asked if they'd like to help me run the workshop. They were both mothers many times over. They knew what I was setting myself up for and, wisely, they weren't going anywhere near it.

Knitting isn't a contact sport, but you would never know it by the number of squabbles exhausted parents mediated while I looked at Laria and wondered exactly what message she was absorbing from this. The Terrible Twos would definitely prove interesting.

Food, however, can work wonders. A well-timed oatmeal-raisin cookie and some string cheese would help restore order to kids and grownups alike. Don't tell anyone, but I dipped into my stash of Chips Ahoy when no one was looking.

"I saw that," a voice said from behind me.

Well, *almost* no one.

"No, you didn't," I said to Wendy with a guilty grin.

"I'm an Oreo girl," she said, "in case anyone asks."

I reached into my secret stash drawer. "I've got you covered." I pulled out one of those little snack packs that I could devour by the dozen.

"By the way, it started to snow a few minutes ago," Wendy said around a mouthful of Oreo.

"Crap," I said, glancing toward the window with dismay. "This is early even for Vermont."

"It's not sticking," Wendy observed. "That's a good sign."

"It's just flurries," I said, clinging to hope.

My cousin, a Maine native, nodded. "You're right. Mother Nature is having a little fun with us."

Twenty minutes later the street in front of the shop was covered in a blanket of snow. The big lazy flakes of a few minutes ago had morphed into the kind of small, persistent downfall that meant we were really in for it.

We take our weather seriously here in northern New England, so a heads-up seemed in order.

The kids, who had been happily chomping away on their snacks, went bat-crap crazy. They ran to the window and started shouting about making snowmen and sledding while the parents gathered up their belongings and tried to monitor the weather conditions on balky cell phones.

The workshop was over.

I asked Wendy if she would take Laria back to the cottage while I stayed behind to close up. The thought of driving through snow with my baby in the car made my blood run as cold as Snow Lake in January.

"Are you sure you'll be okay?"

Wendy knew about my driving-in-snow phobia.

"Okay is stretching it," I said honestly, "but I'll be a lot happier if I know Laria is safe with you."

"I'll stay and help you close up then drive us all back to the cottage."

I shook my head. "Go," I said, giving her a gentle push. "I'll be fine."

Minutes later they were on their way home.

I rang up a significant number of purchases, handed out the goodie bags to everyone, told one and all to help themselves to more juice boxes and cookies for the road. I promised we would reschedule the rest of the workshop in the spring, although I'm not sure how many of the departing attendees would take me up on it.

I also did a lot of apologizing. I apologized for the weather, the beyond quirky cellphone service, the chaos, and the fact that I still had a lot to learn about children.

"Stop it," Mallory said as she paused to thank me for a great afternoon. "Ava and I had an amazing day."

I was almost pathetically grateful for the kind words. "Laria will miss your daughter."

"We'll see you again in the spring," she said with a glance toward the falling snow outside.

"I'm sorry about the snow. I wish that--"

She raised her hand to stop me. "You can't control the weather."

Then again, maybe one day we could. This was Sugar Maple, after all. Of course, I kept that observation to myself.

"Where are you parked?" I asked.

"I'm the old white minivan in front of the coffee shop," she said. "We'll make a run for it."

"You're welcome to an umbrella."

She shook her head. "Thanks, but I'm sure we'll be fine."

I told her I'd hold a good thought for her husband's return home and wished her a safe trip to Rhode Island.

It wasn't until I was locking up the store for the weekend that I realized Mallory had left her phone behind.

Chapter 2

WENDY

I love my cousin. I love her husband. I love their baby more than I can say. I even love the troll warrior who manages their lives and keeps them safe from harm.

But I hate Sugar Maple.

You don't know how good it feels to say that out loud.

I hate Sugar Maple.

The place gives me the creeps. Remember that old science fiction classic, *Invasion of the Body Snatchers*? That's how Sugar Maple makes me feel, like I was seeing only the surface of things, while the real action was happening below my line of vision.

Which, all things considered, is probably true.

Sugar Maple's claim to otherworldly fame was their history of tolerance for the Other. The town had been founded by Chloe's ancestor Aerynn as a refuge for otherworldly beings that were being persecuted by humans. Selkies, trolls, were-families, vampires, house sprites, witches, sorcerers, goblins, and ghosts, all continued to find refuge within the town limits, protected from human mischief.

Too bad it didn't work both ways.

I totally got the fear of humans. I didn't always like us all that much myself. We were capable of great love and compassion, but equally great measures of duplicity and cruelty and violence, as well.

But, given the hype, I still expected more from the Sugar Maples.

So that's why I was surprised when it happened.

I was strapping a bundled-up Laria into her car seat when someone grabbed me from behind.

"Where do you think you're taking that baby?" The voice was female, gruff, more than a little menacing.

I spun around, cracking my head on the doorframe as I did. "Take your hands off me!"

The woman was buried in a huge down parka, her face hidden by scarves and a fur-trimmed hood pulled close. There was something familiar about her but I couldn't come up with a name.

"Where are you going with Laria Hobbs?" she demanded, her fingers still digging into my right shoulder.

"Laria Hobbs *MacKenzie*," I said, pulling away from her. "I'm taking her home where she belongs."

"Don't think I'm not onto you," she said, looming over me like a top-heavy tree about to fall. "You're not going anywhere until I--"

"Verna!" A man's voice stopped her mid-sentence. "There's a blizzard brewing. Let her get that baby home before the storm gets any worse."

Paul Griggs, owner of the hardware store, appeared through a curtain of snow. He was a tall, broad-shouldered man who was the patriarch of the town's only were-family. I knew that Luke considered him a friend, but after what I heard Janice say this morning, I was no longer sure how deep that friendship ran.

His wife glared at him, then turned her anger back in my direction.

"You tell that boyfriend of yours to watch his step," she said, wagging a bony finger under my nose. "We're not going to let a bunch of strangers ruin Sugar Maple."

"You're right." I matched her, glare for glare. "Who needs strangers when you're doing such a great job yourself."

I was shaking by the time I started the car but not from the cold. I had my anger to keep me warm. The baby, however, needed more than that. I turned the heat on full blast.

"Verna Griggs is a jackass," I said as I met Laria's eyes in the rearview mirror. "A total, unmitigated jackass."

I can't swear to it, but I'm pretty sure the baby nodded.

"And he's not my boyfriend," I went on, as I eased my car onto Osborne. "I mean, I'm a little old to have a boyfriend, right?"

The baby reserved judgment on that one.

I refused to consider exactly what my relationship with Gavan might be. And what was a "relationship" anyway? We hadn't slept together. Except for one wildly sexy kiss, we had barely touched. Mostly we talked. Or at least I did. He knew more about me than anyone on this planet. Sometimes I felt like we didn't even need words to communicate our deepest thoughts. The connection between us was as powerful as it was hopeless.

As Chloe had made crystal clear to me on more than one occasion, Gavan's destiny had been decided for him on the day he was born. It was his responsibility to make sure Rohesia's line went forward into the future.

And that could never happen with me.

I was a thirty-year-old, divorced Homo sapiens who had tried for years to get pregnant and failed spectacularly every month.

Not exactly the heroine of any fairy tale I'd ever read, but at least I knew the truth about my situation.

Poor Chloe hadn't a clue.

Chapter 3

CHLOE

I puttered around the shop while I waited to see if Mallory returned for her phone but the sight of the snow, growing heavier by the minute, was making me sick to my stomach with dread and all I wanted was to get safely home as soon as possible.

Superman is afraid he'll stumble over a lump of Kryptonite and lose his superpowers. Janice is afraid of thunderstorms and has been known to hide in her coat closet with her basset hound Barney until the storms pass by. Lynette can't look at a picture of a snake without hyperventilating. (We don't have snakes in Sugar Maple, but I keep a paper bag handy just in case she needs to breathe into it.)

Even my husband Luke, a cop who says nothing scares him unless it's carrying a gun, has been known to go a little green around spiders.

For me, it's snow.

The moment the first flake hits the ground, my imagination goes into overdrive and I see eighteen-wheelers sailing airborne across an eight-lane highway, heading straight for me.

And that's just for starters.

I wished Luke were home from his business trip. The annual meeting of East Coast Chiefs of Police ended today and he was scheduled to fly home from Philadelphia tonight. At least, that was the plan. I crossed my fingers and hoped this unexpected snowstorm was limited to our small dot on the map. There was so much I wanted to tell him about, especially the spat with Janice. I knew he would find her take on Rohesia's clan and the effect they were having on Sugar Maple very enlightening.

I busied myself with some last minute chores, giving Mallory a little more time to make an appearance but it became clear that wasn't going to happen.

I made sure calls to the store would be forwarded to my cell, and then I scribbled a note for Mallory, telling her that I had her phone. I dropped the note into a weatherproof plastic pouch, and taped it to the front door. I slipped the phone into one of my tote bags to take home with me for safekeeping.

The thought of Mallory and Ava driving to Rhode Island without a cell phone unnerved me, but there wasn't anything more I could do. With any luck at all, they would be sipping cocoa with family before Mallory even realized she didn't have her phone with her.

I made sure Penny the cat was settled in and well supplied then tried to text Luke about the snowstorm. I had to hit SEND four times before it went through. (At least, I hoped it went through.) We'd been having a fair bit of trouble lately with power outages, cell phone interruptions, and other annoyances of modern life, which unfortunately coincided with the arrival of Rohesia's clan. Was it possible their brand of Old Magick was somehow screwing with the grid in ways our twenty-first century brand of magick didn't?

I added that to my growing list of worries about the transition.

I was about to text Luke one more time when he called me.

"It's a bad one," he said after bitching about the cellphone connection. "It started here around nine this morning and it shows no sign of letting up any time soon."

A sense of dread washed over me. "Has your flight been cancelled?"

"Not yet," he said, "but I'm pretty sure that's where this is headed. They cut the conference short and we're all going to the airport to try to get out before they shut it down."

I didn't know what was worse: the thought of him trapped in Philly for another day or risking his life to get home.

That was a lie. I definitely knew which option was worse.

"Maybe you should wait it out at the hotel," I said, barely controlling the tremor in my voice. "You can order a big steak from room service and take it easy."

He understood exactly what I was saying and, to my relief, he didn't argue.

"Sounds good," he said, "but it would sound a hell of a lot better if you were here too."

"Sweet talk from a cop?" I said. "I think you miss me."

He told me exactly how much and why. My bones melted.

"Still want me to stay the night in Philly?" he asked.

I looked out the big front window at the rapidly falling snow and sighed. "Yes," I said. "I do." The thought of losing him to a bad decision was more than I could handle. The tiny commuter planes that served the area around Sugar Maple and Boston were scary enough when the skies were clear.

The connection crackled, beeped, and then went flat and silent. I tried his cell but couldn't hold the signal long enough to get through. It took another five minutes for us to reconnect.

I told him a few funny Laria stories that only a parent could fully appreciate and promised to email the videos.

"She misses her daddy," I said. "Every time she hears a male voice, her eyes go wide and she looks around with such a hopeful look on her face."

"I miss both of you," he said, his voice choked with emotion. "I used to be good at this convention stuff." He cleared his throat. "Not so much any more."

I waited while he regrouped then told him about my fight with Janice.

"I'm not surprised," he said. "I've been fielding a dozen complaints a day about Rohesia's ... people."

People? I didn't correct him. I wasn't sure how to refer to them either.

"What kinds of complaints?" I asked.

"Harassment. Minor vandalism. You name it, somebody has complained about it." His laugh was mirthless. "You didn't make many fans with your decision to open Sugar Maple to them."

"That's exactly what Janice told me this morning."

"I wondered how long it would take her to start pounding you about this."

"Why didn't you tell me?" I asked.

"Because so far I haven't been able to prove any of the complaints."

"That's a good thing, isn't it?"

"There's more," he said. "I think their magick is screwing up the power grid. It's affecting Wi-Fi networks and power sources in Pine Notch, Birch Hollow, Green Grove, and as far away as Mountain Ridge. Whatever they're doing, they need to stop ASAP."

"I don't think they're doing anything specifically to screw with our electronics," I said. "I don't think they even know what generates our power."

"That's even worse," Luke said. "Maybe you could devise a stronger spell to keep it all under control for the time being."

"Unfortunately I still don't understand the way their magick operates," I admitted. "Lilith and I have been working on a spell that would contain the energies within our town limits, but we're not there yet."

"Remember Joe Randazzo?"

"That's one heck of a non sequitur," I said.

"Do you remember him?"

I barely suppressed a major eye roll. "Like I could forget the most annoying man in Vermont." Randazzo was head of the County Board of Supervisors and a major thorn in Sugar Maple's side.

"He fielded some complaints about a large group of homeless

24

men, women, and children camping in the woods around Sugar Maple. They were described as wearing robes and blankets and looking like members of a cult."

I groaned loudly. "I thought Rohesia understood they needed to lie low for the time being."

"She might understand the problem, but she hasn't done anything about it. Ask Wendy if Gavan can convince them they need to stay away from strangers until they get up to speed with the twenty-first century."

My husband had a point. It was hard to blend in when you dressed like runaways from a Renaissance Festival.

"I'll try," I said, "but no promises. Wendy's been a little pre-occupied lately."

I wasn't sure if the sound I heard was a snort or a problem with the connection. My money, however, was on the former.

"Speaking of Wendy," he said, "did she make it to your work-shop before the snow started?"

"She showed up at ten a.m., sharp," I said, pausing for dramatic effect. "Twenty seconds later so did Gavan."

"What do you think is going on with those two?"

"Pretty much the same thing you think is going on."

"Whatever," he said. "I'm glad she's there. Let her drive you and the baby home."

"And leave the car here?"

"We'll dig it out in the spring."

I laughed out loud. "Too late. I sent Wendy home with the baby an hour ago."

"Why didn't you go with them?"

"I had to close up."

"She couldn't stay and help out?"

"Luke, she offered but I told her to go." I was a mother now. Making sure our daughter got safely home was paramount.

"So why are you still there?"

"Is this an interrogation?" I shot back. I told him about Mallory and the forgotten cell phone. "I was giving her a chance to double back for it."

"Unless she's crazy, she won't be coming back for anything," he said. "This is going to be a bad one. You've waited long enough. You need to go home."

Home.

I would never get tired of hearing that word.

"You're right," I said.

"Text Wendy when you're on your way," he said, "and then text me when you get there. If you have any trouble, blueflame Paul Griggs. He has a truck with a snowplow. He'll come and get you."

After what Janice had told me about the anger brewing in Sugar Maple, I wasn't so sure of that, but telling Luke the rest of the gossip could wait until later.

Romance isn't always flowers and chocolates. I had spent most of my adult life immersing myself in romantic movies, romance novels, and silly love songs. My idea of true love had been tied up with grand gestures and flowery pronouncements that were more for social media than they were for real life. Who would have guessed that sometimes the most romantic thing a man could do was worry about you?

By the time I finally turned out the lights at Sticks & Strings, it was clear Luke was right. This wasn't going to be an ordinary snowstorm. The winds had picked up significantly, whipping the heavy downfall into an aggressive adversary whose main purpose was making sure you couldn't see a foot in front of you.

"What the heck is going on?" I muttered as I waited for the car to warm up. This was leaf-peeping season, not ski season. I had thought I would have at least a few more weeks before I had to start my annual worrying.

Snow was beautiful, but it wasn't my friend. I had lost my parents in an auto accident on an icy road when I was six years old. Our daughter Laria came into this world in the back of our SUV during a terrible snowstorm ten months ago. The persistent sound of heavy snow lashing against the car windows was quickly getting under my skin.

Don't get me wrong. I like making snowmen and having snowball fights as much as the next person. I also like sitting by the window with a pot of hot chocolate and a lapful of knitting, watching those big, beautiful white flakes turn our landscape into a wonderland. I'm a Vermonter, born and bred, and I celebrate all the good things every other Vermonter associates with snow: skiing; skating; snowboarding; and sledding.

But when it comes to climbing behind the wheel of my car and heading out onto the skating rink known as the streets of Sugar Maple, all bets are off.

I start to sweat. My hands shake. I gasp for air like I'm breathing underwater.

And that was while the car was still in park.

I'm not exaggerating when I say my old Buick was built like a tank. This was one of those "they don't make 'em like that any more" vehicles people joke about but secretly admire. At least, that was what I told myself. Unfortunately it wasn't built to drive through a blizzard with a freaked-out driver behind the wheel. I shifted into drive and eased onto Good Way. I was pathetically happy to see I was the only fool on the road.

Our cottage was at the opposite side of town, at the edge of the woods. Although it was less than a ten-minute drive in good weather, this time I wasn't sure I'd make it home before nightfall.

The shops were all closed tight against the storm. No tourists anywhere to be found. Not even a low-flying spirit en route to the Inn. My windshield wipers had a hard time keeping up with the relentless fall of snow obscuring my vision. No doubt about it: we were fast approaching whiteout conditions. Snow brought with it a combination of beauty and treachery that would have been seductive if it didn't scare the daylights out of me the way it did.

I ignored stop signs. I was alone on the road and those skidding, sliding stops made my stomach turn inside out. Besides, I was married to the chief of police and I was reasonably sure I could talk myself out of a ticket if I had to. I was willing to take that chance. Especially since Luke was also the entire police force.

It was slow going through the snow-hushed, soundless town. My tires struggled to gain purchase. Familiar landmarks seemed to appear and disappear through the thick curtain of blowing snow. It felt like I was the only one left in a vast, icy world.

Every winter you hear a story about a family who got stranded during a blizzard with only their car for shelter. I devoured those stories. I even took notes. What would I do in the same situation? Did I have what it took to survive?

Which was probably why you'd find reflective blankets, flares, kitty litter, bottled water, and freeze-dried beef stew in my trunk in July.

Okay. I admit it. I get a little melodramatic when it comes to snow and ice but there was no denying the slow trickle of sweat working its way down my spine as I white-knuckled my way toward home. I actually considered sliding into some snow-laden hedges and calling Paul to drive me home.

I slid onto Osborne and slowly rolled toward home. Our cottage was nestled at the edge of the woods, just deep enough to be nicely secluded from nosy neighbors. It was one of the first structures built in Sugar Maple, long before we had a bustling business district that brought in tourists. And long before we had paved roadways.

It was only mid-afternoon, but the town was shut down tight. The tourists had fled for the safety of motel rooms in adjacent towns, hunkering down for the duration. Our townspeople, usually no slouches when it came to storm management, were nowhere to be seen. There was something downright apocalyptic about the scene that set my nerves on edge.

The fact that I couldn't get a signal on my smartphone didn't help matters. I had tried to text Wendy before I left to let her know I was on my way, but the signal was non-existent. Despite the fact that Sugar Maple was pretty much situated in the middle of nowhere and surrounded by mountains, our cell service had always been pretty good. Or at least it had until Rohesia and her clan arrived.

Luke was right. I had been treading softly with the newcomers, cutting them some slack as they tried to fall into step with the strange new world in which they found themselves. I needed to redouble my efforts to either tame their Old World powers or help them adapt those powers to our 21st century world. Either way, they couldn't keep screwing up the grid or it wouldn't be long before our secret was out.

I was thinking about Joe Randazzo, the county supervisor, and how much he would love to nail us on even the most minor infraction when something, or someone, appeared in the road about ten feet in front of me.

The figure was swathed in pale, billowing fabric. Its face was hidden from view. Even though I knew better, my foot hit the brake hard in a very human reflexive action. The car slid sideways and moments before it made contact, the figure merged with the falling snow and disappeared.

"Damn," I muttered, forcing my hands to release their death grip on the steering wheel. The car was now perpendicular to the road, front bumper almost kissing a giant maple tree. I was shaking so hard I could hear my teeth rattling inside my head. Were Rohesia's people practical jokers or had the individual been trying to scare me into an accident? Of course, there was the possibility that whoever or whatever it was had wandered away from their settlement and had been every bit as scared as I had been by the encounter.

The only thing I knew for sure was that I wasn't laughing. I could have hit that tree and been killed, leaving my daughter motherless the same way I had been.

Not for the first time, I wondered if I had made a mistake opening up Sugar Maple to Rohesia's clan, a group whose understanding of our 21st century earthbound dimension was non-existent. When my mother agreed to betroth me to Gavan on my sixth birthday, her intention had been to ensure both my future security and that of the creatures of Sugar Maple. Linking our clans through a dynastic marriage must have seemed a foolproof way to secure my birthright.

My mother had no way of knowing she wouldn't live out the day or that, years later, her daughter would fall in love with a human, same as she had, and set out to make a life with him.

Had I made the decision to bring Rohesia's clan into our dimension out of guilt or a sense of duty? I wasn't sure it mattered but the question lingered just the same. Still, they were here and it was up to me to figure out how to make it work before the entire town turned against me.

First, however, I had to get home.

I struggled to get the Buick back on the road and facing in the right direction. Even though I was close to the cottage, the fear of being alone in a storm set my nerves on edge. There were some things not even magick could overcome and nature was one of them. Thanks to my human ingenuity and a humongous bag of kitty litter in my trunk, I finally managed the task.

My cottage can be reached only by a dirt road that veers off from Osborne at the edge of the woods. In fact, calling it a road is giving it too much credit. Path is more like it. In fact, if you didn't know the path was there, you would never find it.

The tire tracks left by Wendy's van an hour ago were rapidly filling with snow. I followed in their wake, slipping and sliding, up the slight rise that led to the cottage.

Lights burned brightly in the windows. Curls of smoke rose from the brick chimney and disappeared into the swirling snow.

The ten-minute drive had taken forty-three minutes but I was home safe.

Well, almost.

I had told Wendy to park her faded minivan in the driveway, as close to the front door as possible, to limit the baby's exposure to the wind-blown snow. I parked the ancient Buick at the foot of the driveway, turned off the engine, and swore I wouldn't drive again until the spring solstice.

As much as I missed Luke, I was glad he had opted to stay another night in Philadelphia. Before long both the highways and our twisty, narrow local roads would be thick with snow and ice. The thought made my blood run colder than the wind that propelled me up the driveway.

I was halfway to the front door when I heard a loud crack to my right and before I could react, something hard and cold and wet hit me in the head and sent me tumbling into the accumulating snow.

Chapter 4

MALLORY

"Laria can fly."

Six years of motherhood had pretty much prepared Mallory Dawson Grant for everything. She didn't miss a beat.

"A flying baby?" She cast a quick glance at her daughter Ava in the rearview mirror as she rolled to a stop at the traffic light near the entrance to the highway. "That's pretty cool."

Ava nodded. "Her daddy doesn't like it, but it makes her mommy laugh."

"How do you know Laria can fly?" Mallory asked. "Did you see her fly?"

"No," said Ava. "She told me."

Imagination was a wonderful thing, but Mallory knew there was a fine line between storytelling and lying.

"I didn't know Laria could talk. Sounds like she's a pretty smart baby."

"Yes," said Ava, "she is. But she only talks to me."

"And why is that?"

She caught a glimpse of tiny shrugged shoulders. "Because I can hear her."

"Can't her mommy hear her?"

"I don't know."

The light changed to green. Mallory's breath hissed as her tires struggled for purchase on the snowy roadway. It had taken an hour to travel the fifteen miles between Sugar Maple and the highway that would take them south to Rhode Island. A gas station and a pair of fast food restaurants beckoned near the entrance to the highway. Time to make an executive decision.

"Bathroom check," she called over her shoulder. "This might be our last chance before we get to Grandma and Grandpa's house."

"Yes," Ava said, nodding her head vigorously. "And hot chocolate."

"First the hot chocolate, then the bathroom." A small distinction, but an important one when the car trip ahead would be measured in hours, not minutes.

Of course, they ended up with more than hot chocolate. She purchased a Happy Meal for Ava and splurged on a Big Mac with fries for herself. The inside of the restaurant was well-lighted and warm and for a few minutes Mallory forgot about the snow slapping against the big windows.

Josh's parents would be so surprised when they pulled into their driveway and beeped the horn. Trish and Allen were both retired teachers in the early stages of what-do-we-do-next. They had been thinking about part-time tutoring but hadn't yet pulled the trigger.

She loved her in-laws, even more now that her own parents were gone. She wanted Ava to spend as much time with them as possible. Grandparents were important, especially when your father was stationed on the other side of the earth. It scared Mallory to think of how few people stood between her daughter and a dangerous world. If something happened to Josh or to her, she knew Trish and Allen would guide Ava into adulthood, but she wasn't going to let it come to that. Not if she could help it.

Even though it was still early days, she and Josh had decided to tell his parents that she was pregnant again. Conceiving Ava had been a miracle. Getting pregnant a second time? That was the stuff of dreams, even if it had happened the night before he had deployed to Afghanistan. Unexpected. Wonderful. Very scary. Fortunately, Boston was a short drive from her in-laws' home in Rhode Island and she had an appointment Tuesday at Brigham with a high-risk pregnancy expert.

There wasn't a scrap of wood in the entire restaurant, so she knocked on the tabletop.

"Why did you do that, Mommy?"

Her Ava never missed a trick.

"Just a superstition, honey."

The child's brow crinkled. "What's that?"

"Something you do because you've always done it." *And you're afraid that if you quit doing it, the world will stop spinning on its axis.*

"Why?"

"For good luck."

"Why do you need good luck?"

"Everyone needs good luck."

Ava considered that for a moment. "What's luck?"

"It's like when you find a quarter on the ground and you weren't looking for it."

Ava nodded, her small face serious. "Can I have one of your fries, please?"

Another lesson in motherhood. Never volunteer more information than your kid is actually looking for. Mallory hoped she remembered that when it was time for the *where do babies come from* talk.

"Where's your flower?" Mallory asked. "Did you put it in your pocket?" The crocheted hot pink accessory was one of her daughter's favorite things.

"I gave it to Laria."

"You did?" Mallory was surprised. Ava loved the yarn flower so much that she even wore it when she slept. "What made you do that?"

"She said she liked it."

"That was very generous of you, Ava."

Her daughter nodded. "I know."

She would whip up another one for her girl tomorrow.

They finished their meals, paid a visit to the bathroom, and were about to leave when Mallory decided to check for messages.

"Tell me this isn't happening," she said, her voice shaking.

Ava looked on, eyes wide with curiosity, as Mallory fumbled through her pockets. She emptied the contents of her enormous purse on a cleared table, pushing her way through socks-in-progress, two copies of Vogue Knitting, her wallet, a juice box, a bag of oatmeal raisin cookies, coloring books, crayons, and three packets of tissues.

"Mommy?" Ava's voice was high with concern. "What are you looking for?"

"My phone." Mallory managed to sound calmer than she felt. "I can't find it."

"I bet it's in the car," Ava said. "Remember when the water bottle rolled under the seat that time?"

The car! Of course it was in the car. Where else would it be?

Except it wasn't. For once the interior of the minivan was free from clutter.

"Daddy says the best way to find something is to think back to all the places you remember seeing it."

A sharp spear of longing pierced Mallory's heart but she pushed it aside and stayed focused. Military spouses were good at that.

"I had the phone in the knit shop," she said out loud. "I changed our outgoing message just before the workshop started and saw the battery was getting low." She groaned. "I asked Chloe if I could plug it in to recharge."

And then she had totally forgotten all about it.

There was no way she was going to brave the highway during a snowstorm with no phone and a six year old in the back seat. Like it or not, she had to go back to Sugar Maple and retrieve her phone.

Mallory was a snow country girl. Born and raised in upstate New York, she had grown up so close to the Canadian border that her first word was *hockey*. Navigating through snow was second nature to her. She knew the drill. Slow down. Concentrate. Keep a light foot on the brake and be prepared to steer into a skid. Make sure you have a bag of kitty litter in the trunk, some reflective blankets, flares, flashlights, batteries, bottles of water, a few protein bars. You would probably never need any of those things, but it didn't hurt to be prepared.

That was what you did from November until May and you didn't think twice about it.

But it was the second Saturday in October. The weather forecast hadn't even whispered rain, much less snow.

And she hadn't given a single thought to the unexpected.

So now there she was in the middle of a Vermont blizzard with her daughter in the back seat and no water, no blankets, no kitty litter in the trunk, and no cell phone.

The roads weren't great but they were still open. She wasn't sure that would be the case an hour from now, but so far, so good. The trip back seemed to be taking a long time, but given the reduced visibility and speed, that was understandable.

The miles slowly accumulated beneath her wheels as she kept moving back toward Sugar Maple. She consoled herself with the fact that she was far closer to town than she was to the highway. Slow but steady, she told herself. It seemed like they had been on the road forever, but she was making progress.

Something up ahead caught her eye and she slowed down to a crawl. A fallen tree the size of a T-Rex completely blocked the two-lane road from shoulder to shoulder.

"Why did we stop?" Ava asked from the back seat.

"There's a tree blocking the road."

Ava squirmed in her car seat, trying to see. "Where?"

"Right in front of us."

"What are we going to do?"

Good question.

"Stay put," she said. "I'm getting out of the car so I can look around."

The snow stung her skin like shrapnel and she was shocked to realize the accumulation already went halfway to her knees. For one crazy moment, she considered abandoning her phone altogether and heading back toward civilization but she had to be within shouting distance of Sugar Maple and a warm place to spend the night.

She spotted what appeared to be some kind of path or roadway about twenty yards back. It was worth a shot. The path had to lead somewhere. A house, maybe, or a short cut to a bigger road that would take her to Sugar Maple or one of the other nearby towns. What other choice was there? The snow was getting deeper and she would never be able to retrace her steps back to the highway entrance. And sitting in a freezing car, praying that help would somehow find them was not an option.

It took every ounce of snow-driving experience and an awesome vehicle with blessed all-wheel drive, but she finally managed to back up to the path and start moving forward again.

She grinned at Ava in the rear-view mirror. "Now that's what a woman driver can do!" she said, feeling more than a little pleased with herself.

Ava was engrossed in watching a video and paid no attention.

One day she would understand.

The only thing that kept the path even remotely identifiable was the canopy of trees overhead, deflecting some of the accumulation. She had always prided herself on her sense of direction but this time she was stumped. North. South. East. West. She had no idea which direction she was headed and no landmarks to guide her.

"I'd kill for a working GPS," she muttered, relaxing her grip on the wheel a little. The glow of her headlights made the falling snow glitter like precious gems as she moved steadily forward. "I shouldn't have turned back."

"What, Mommy?" Ava piped up from behind her.

"I said I shouldn't have turned back, honey. I should have found a Best Buy, bought a burner phone, and then hopped onto the highway."

"But you didn't," Ava said, with the practical logic of a six-year-old.

"No, I didn't," Mallory agreed, "so now it's time for Plan B."

In the back seat, Ava giggled. "Daddy says Plan B means Plan A sucks."

"Ava!" She was trying hard not to giggle herself. "Don't say 'sucks.'"

"Daddy does."

"Daddy can. You can't."

She didn't have to see her daughter's face to know there was some major sulking going on.

"We'll stay in Sugar Maple tonight," she said in as relaxed a tone as she could manage. "We'll have a good sleep, eat a big breakfast in the morning, then drive down to Rhode Island to Grandma and Grandpa's house after they plow the roads."

"Can we stay with Laria?"

"We're not going to bother Laria. We'll just ask her mommy for our phone and say thanks."

"I want to finish showing Laria how to knit."

"Maybe next time."

"When next time?"

Take a deep breath, Mallory. Count to ten. "The next time Chloe schedules a workshop."

"When will that be?"

"I don't know."

"Can you ask?"

"After I find my phone."

Ava thought about that for a moment. "That makes good sense."

Mallory's irritation ebbed as quickly as it had flowed. "Thank you," she said. "I'm glad you think so."

"I liked knitting."

"I liked it, too, when I was your age."

"When was that?"

Mallory grinned into the rearview mirror. "A long time ago."

"How long?"

"You have a lot of questions tonight."

"I know," she said. "I'm curious."

"Twenty-eight years ago," Mallory said.

"Twenty-eight plus six," Ava said, a question in her voice.

"Can you add those numbers together?"

"It's a big number."

"Yes, it is," Mallory said, laughing. "Definitely a big number."

They drove in silence for a few minutes. She wished she had a map so she could get an idea how deep the woods around Sugar Maple were. It felt like she had been driving through them for hours. She glanced down at the gas gauge and winced.

Concentrate on driving, Mallory. You can worry about filling the tank in the morning.

First she left her phone behind at Sticks & Strings. Then she forgot to top off the gas tank at the station right next to the McDonald's where they'd stopped to eat. Normally she had the bits and pieces of life under control, mainly because she had no choice. With Josh in Afghanistan, she was operating as a single parent, which meant there was no room for error. She wasn't a control freak, but she did find comfort in knowing she was in charge.

Not that she felt in charge at the moment.

The woods seemed to go on forever. Even taking the blinding snowstorm into account, she should have stumbled onto Sugar Maple by now. She silently cursed the downed tree that had sent her in this direction.

"Why did the man run away?" Ava's high-pitched voice broke the silence.

Mallory frowned and glanced in the rearview mirror. "I didn't see anyone."

"Back there," Ava said, squirming around so she could look out the back window. "He was waving at us."

Her daughter had been blessed with an active imagination. Sometimes Mallory found it difficult to distinguish facts from flights of fancy.

"Did you wave back?"

"I wanted to, but he ran away."

"Where did he go?"

"Back into the woods."

"I bet he'll be happy to get home."

"Maybe he lives in the woods."

"Maybe he does," she said, glancing back at her daughter in the rearview mirror. "I hope he stays warm."

"He will," Ava said with great certainty.

At her daughter's age, Mallory had been shy and cautious, certain only of her own name. This child was pure Josh, all confidence and a touch of swagger. The trick was making sure she stayed that way.

She couldn't wait to tell him about their daughter's latest observations. How had military spouses managed before email and Skype, smartphones and FaceTime? She tried to imagine long-distance family life limited to snail mail and the thought made her sad. Life was too short to be separated from the ones you loved most. She hated that Josh was missing out on Ava's daily life, the small things that bind a family together.

"Rats!" she muttered. What if he tried calling her and was sent to voicemail? Thanks to the time difference between Afghanistan and the east coast, they usually connected in the middle of the night.

She was bent low over the wheel, peering through the windshield, as a tall, shadowy figure darted in front of the car, barely visible through the thick curtain of falling snow. She hit the brake hard. The car fishtailed wildly, swinging out across the narrow, snow-covered road, and then headed straight for a stand of maples.

Chapter 5

CHLOE

Here's the thing about snow: you never know when it's going to turn on you. You could be driving along, minding your own business, and bam! You hit a slippery patch and slam into a tree. Or maybe you're trying to shovel a path to your front door when you push a little too hard and a heart attack takes you out before you draw your next breath.

A frosting of snow on Christmas Eve is magical.

A blizzard in early October? Not so much.

Believe me, the last thing I'd expected was for one of the sugar maples lining my driveway to snap a mid-sized limb and send it sailing into the side of my head. I stumbled, then dropped to my knees, dizzy and disoriented, like I'd polished off a couple of margaritas on an empty stomach. Drops of blood appeared on the blanket of white. I touched my hand to my right temple and came away with a smear of bright red.

Head wounds bleed like crazy. We all know that. But when the blood is yours it takes on a whole other reality.

I stumbled into the cottage and made my way to the kitchen. Wendy shrieked when she saw me while Elspeth dropped a soup ladle onto the floor with a clatter. My baby daughter, however, crowed with delight and clapped her hands at the sight of her mother looking like a skinny, snow-covered Sasquatch. The blood trickling down the side of my face didn't bother her at all. She was strapped into her high chair, gumming handfuls of broccoli and buttered spaghetti, while she watched the goings-on with great interest.

"I think she's enjoying this a little too much," I said, as I dripped snow on the kitchen floor. "She's laughing her head off at me!"

I winced as Elspeth dabbed at my face with a clean towel.

"Your daughter is in love with snow," Wendy said as she handed me a pair of yoga pants and one of Luke's old BU sweatshirts she'd found in the dryer. "You should have seen her looking out the car window when we drove home. She was mesmerized."

I stepped out of my soaking wet jeans and hand-knit sweater and slipped into the warm, dry clothing.

Wendy scooped up the snow-soaked items, casting a rueful glance at my once-beautiful sweater. "I'm not sure even your magick can save this one."

It was a slouchy pullover I'd knitted in thousands of yards of fingering weight silk blend that I wasn't ready to part with.

"I was hoping you'd see what you can do," I said. "A good soak and blocking can work wonders."

My cousin didn't seem convinced but I had confidence. She was the best blocker I'd ever met.

Elspeth bustled into the room, carrying a bowl of warm, herb-scented water.

"Don't be delaying," she warned me as she placed the bowl on the kitchen table. "The sooner I apply the brew, the sooner you be healed." She motioned for me to sit down at the table and I obeyed. I knew better than to argue with a troll on a mission.

Her hands were gnarled but amazingly capable. She removed the temporary bandage she had applied to stop the bleeding with one swift motion then set about holding a warm, wet poultice against the spot where the tree branch had done its damage.

I winced as the highly fragrant liquid seeped into my skin. "I never thought one of our trees would turn on me."

"You're lucky you weren't seriously hurt," Wendy said. "That was a pretty big limb that clipped you."

"Don't remind me," I said. "And here I thought driving was the dangerous part."

"Luke said you were going to call and let us know when you were on your way," Wendy remarked. She had taken up a spot at the kitchen stove, stirring a humongous pot of chicken noodle soup. The aroma wafting through the room was downright intoxicating. "We would have been watching for you."

"I tried to, but I couldn't get cell service."

"That explains why I couldn't get through to you either." Wendy gave the pot another brisk stir, then put down the spoon and joined us at the table. "I guess the storm is causing trouble."

"It's not just the storm," I said, wincing again as Elspeth continued her ministrations. "Rohesia and her crowd aren't helping matters."

"That couldn't be – oh!" Wendy ducked as Laria lobbed a chubby fistful of spaghetti with mashed broccoli her way. "You almost got me, girl!"

Laria giggled and went back to gumming her meal, clearly enjoying the dinner show.

"A stubborn lot they be," Elspeth said as she finished treating my injury. "The old one, she wouldn't be much for change."

"That's not true!" Wendy exclaimed. "Gavan says Rohesia wants this transition to work and is willing to compromise."

"She has a funny way of showing it." I pushed aside the list of troubles Janice had recounted earlier at the shop. "To be honest, I'd be happy if they would just rein in their magick before it takes down the entire power grid." I glanced over at my cousin. "Luke was hoping you'd talk to Gavan about it."

"If there's a problem, it isn't Gavan," Wendy said, surprising no one. "He's doing his best to make them understand." She plucked a piece of broccoli from the floor beneath Laria's high chair. "They're still living the way they did in their other dimension. The things we take for granted are alien magick to them."

Elspeth shot her a quizzical look. "You and the boy be saying a lot it seems."

Wendy's cheeks reddened. "I'm just trying to explain our world to him."

Elspeth and I locked eyes.

"We're not blind, Wendy," I said. "We all know what's going on."

"Nothing is going on," my cousin said through locked jaws. "Nothing *can* go on. Aren't you the ones who've told me that at least a hundred times?"

I didn't have the energy to repeat all the reasons why happily-ever-after wasn't in the cards for them, so I stuck with the issue at hand.

"The problem has gone beyond the Sugar Maple town limits," I said. "Luke told me that the surrounding towns are starting to report frequent power outages and cable disruptions. If we don't figure something out fast, we'll have all of Vermont showing up to investigate." I didn't have to explain why that wasn't a good prospect.

"I'm from the human world," Wendy said, brightening. "Maybe I can talk directly to Rohesia—"

"There are those what don't believe in following rules," Elspeth interrupted. "She be too old to change is what I'm thinking."

Elspeth had visited the newcomers twice that I knew of in an attempt to ease their transition to our realm of existence. It had seemed a logical pairing. Elspeth was easily as old as Rohesia, but unlike the newcomer, Elspeth had spent her life in the human realm. She understood rules and boundaries and what was required to live within the human community. I should have realized the two powerful magicks from different clans would clash sooner or later. Unfortunately, Elspeth had the sensibilities of a marine drill sergeant, while Rohesia's sense of entitlement was most often seen in British royalty and government bureaucrats.

Not exactly a match made in heaven.

"Maybe so, but I understand why they're struggling," Wendy said. "I'm a human from this realm and I still find it hard to understand what the rules are here in Sugar Maple."

"The rules are pretty much the same here as they are in Bailey's Harbor," I said. "Can you be more specific?"

She gestured toward the storm howling outside the cottage. "The blizzard, for instance. I saw a snow blower in your garage. Why don't you just magick the snow away? That's what I would do if I had your powers."

Elspeth turned away from the loaf of homemade bread she had been slicing, "There be no tricks when it comes to the natural world. We live within it, not above."

"Elspeth is right," I said. "Even if we could impact the weather – and I don't know that we can, even if we wanted to – that would work against us in the long run. We want to blend in with the humans, not stand out."

Wendy thought about it for a moment then nodded. "I guess it wouldn't make much sense for the rest of Vermont to be buried in ten feet of snow while the residents of Sugar Maple are running around in shorts and tank tops."

The image of Midge Stallworth, our resident vampire funeral director, strutting around in shorts and a tank top made me laugh out loud.

"'Twould be easier on the other side of the mist," Elspeth mused as she took a stick of butter from the refrigerator. "To hide who you are is a burden to all."

"So why do you stay here?" Wendy asked. "You must have options."

"This realm be all I know from birth, missy, same as you. 'Tis Rohesia and the Others I speak of. There be some as believe coming here was a mistake. They think they should have stayed where they began and ended there when it did."

Wendy, who had clearly been spending considerable time around the Others shook her head. "Gavan told me that the younger members are eager to build lives here among mortals, but they aren't exactly being welcomed by their Sugar Maple peers. They want to be part of our world."

"There be much to learn before that happens," Elspeth said. "Traps abound."

"Elspeth is right," I said. "Sugar Maple has survived this long because we learned how to adapt to the world we live in, not because we tried to change it."

Laria rapped one of her fists on the highchair tray and we all laughed.

"That one be too big for her britches," Elspeth observed with a twinkle in her eye. "'Tis a trait you humans share."

"Better be careful, Elspeth," I teased. "The humans in this room outnumber you three to one."

"The wee one be leaving her human self behind soon, I'm thinking. Her magick grows faster than she does."

Good news to Elspeth, but a mixed blessing to me. I wanted my daughter to embrace both sides of her heritage but the rapid development of her magickal side might make that unlikely.

Maybe it had something to do with the centuries she'd lived and the things she'd seen, but Elspeth held most of the human race in something perilously close to contempt. Apparently miracles still happened, because the venerable warrior troll had opened her heart to both Luke and to Wendy in a way that continued to surprise us all.

Laria giggled and munched on buttery broccoli. Elspeth kept a sharp but loving eye on her charge. Wendy served up bowls of insanely fragrant chicken noodle soup with chunks of warm, fresh bread on the side. I could feel myself relaxing with each bite of bread and spoonful of soup I scarfed down.

If Luke had been here with us instead of in Philadelphia, life would have been perfect.

Not that long ago I was living alone in the cottage with my four beloved felines, a bag of Chips Ahoy and Netflix. My magick was non-existent and the future seemed bleak at best. Toward the end of Sex and the City's run on television, Carrie Bradshaw spoke about her loneliness. "The loneliness is palpable," she said and that was how it had been for me. Loneliness was next to me when I fell asleep to Jimmy Fallon, and it was waiting for me when I woke up to the Today Show crew. All my life I had yearned for a family like the ones I saw on television and in movies, for the connections the rest of the world took for granted. I wanted to fill the cottage with people I loved who loved me back.

I might as well have been wishing for the moon.

It had seemed an impossible dream for a half-human, half-magick knitter who could count her second dates on one hand and have four fingers left over, but sometimes the Universe has a surprise up her sleeve.

I was living the life I had dreamed of. I had a husband and a baby. I had Elspeth, a link to my family's past and my daughter's future. I had my cousin Wendy, a living, breathing link to my human father and the human side of my lineage.

I loved and was loved in return. Blizzard or no blizzard, could life get any better?

And then the phone rang.

Chapter 6

MALLORY

"Hold on, honey," Mallory said to her daughter a second before the crash. "Don't be afraid. We're going to feel a little bump."

"Mommy?" Ava's voice was small, scared.

She had never lied to her daughter before. A little bump? Oh, god, please let it be a little bump. She leaned forward, trying to see what was happening. The snow would cushion things, right? Like a big soft white pillow that--

The explosion echoed in her ears as something hit her fast and hard, knocking her back in her seat. Pain shot through her head, her left side, and into the center of her body, effectively shutting down her brain.

She gasped for breath. Smoke was everywhere. A heavy chemical stink filled her head, making her eyes water. The back of her throat burned like she had swallowed a lit match.

Nothing made sense. She tried to speak but couldn't grasp the words she needed.

The world tumbled around her. She didn't know if she was

sitting up, lying down, or flying through space. Nausea flooded through her, worse than any morning sickness she had ever known.

Snow . . . a detour . . . someone standing in the road . . . the hard, unyielding tree . . . an explosion of white followed by pain—

Ava! Oh god, where was Ava?

Faces peered in through the windows, staring at her, mumbling things she couldn't understand. Was this how it felt to die? Were they there to guide her into some shadowy afterlife?

Help my daughter! Please help her!

Her fingers struggled with the shoulder harness but they weren't cooperating with her brain. Warm, sticky liquid splashed onto her hands as she fumbled with the buckle. She was bleeding. She could feel it, taste it. She retched hard and a deep pain tore through her mid-section.

The faces at the window recoiled, moving back into the shadows.

"Help her," she whispered into the darkness. "Please . . . some-body . . . help!"

But Ava was nowhere to be found.

Suddenly she was awake in every cell and fiber of her body. Adrenaline burned through her veins, flooding her with super-human strength. She tore the shoulder harness from its mounting and opened the door, throwing her body into the storm.

"Ava!" she cried as she struggled to push her way through the snow, desperate to get to her daughter. "Ava, talk to me!"

She was only six years old, just a baby. Her life had barely begun. It had to be a dream . . . a terrible dream . . . one of those nightmares that made you desperate to wake up . . . except it was real. She wasn't in her warm bed. She was fighting a blizzard in the middle of nowhere with a baby growing inside her belly and her daughter slipping away, just beyond reach.

The adrenaline rush was gone. Her legs gave way beneath her and she slumped into the snow. Despair sent her spiraling down, down, down—

"Wake up, Mommy!"

Ava's high, sweet voice in her ear.

"Please, Mommy! Come back!"

Soft hands against her cheek.

Was it possible?

She opened her eyes, lashes heavy with wet snow. Ava's beautiful little face swam into view, blurry and doubled, but wonderfully, miraculously, alive.

"Oh, Ava!" She struggled to sit upright in the snow, pulling her daughter toward her. "Oh, baby, you're still here!"

Ava shivered in her arms. "The bag blew up at you. I was scared but it went away."

What bag? What was her daughter talking about?

"I—I don't understand."

"The bag hit you," Ava explained, voice shaking. "Then smelly smoke came out and I couldn't see."

She tried to nod but the motion made her stomach lurch. "The air bag," she managed, finally understanding. "That's a good thing. It saved me from being hurt."

"But you *are* hurt," her very literal daughter observed. "Your face is bleeding."

More of the world came back to Mallory as she glanced toward the minivan, crumpled and spewing steam into the snow-heavy sky. They weren't going back to Sugar Maple or anywhere else tonight. She wasn't sure if it was late afternoon or early evening. The world around her was white with snow, snow, and more snow. Ava shivered again and Mallory tried to figure out what her next move should be. Why was it so hard to do something so simple?

"Get up, mommy." Ava tugged at her arm. "It's cold."

Mallory nodded, trying desperately to untangle the thoughts and images snaking through her brain. They should call 911 for help. That was the first thing they should do.

Ava tried to help her stand up but Mallory's balance was shaky at best and she stumbled more than walked the few feet back to the car. Faint bursts of steam rose from the damaged front end but the engine was ominously quiet.

The sliding passenger side door was wide open and she frowned.

"How did you get out?" she asked her daughter through the fog that had settled over her brain. The door lock had a childproof option that Mallory relied upon.

"They helped me."

"I don't understand."

"The people in fancy bathrobes," her daughter said, scrambling into the back seat of the white minivan. "They opened the door and undid the strap for me."

"The door was locked," Mallory said, closing her eyes against a wave of dizziness. "This doesn't make sense."

Moving slowly against a rising tide of pain, Mallory eased herself onto the back seat next to her daughter. Poor Ava was shivering like a baby bird. She tried to wrap her arms around the child, but the pain in her chest and side was too great and she yelped when she lifted her arms.

"Mommy? Is anybody going to help us?"

Her thoughts tumbled through her brain. Flashes of images danced before her eyes, but nothing made sense. Breathe, she told herself. Take a deep breath and start again.

The phone! Her spirits rose. All she had to do was press 9-1-1 and help would be on the way.

"I need my tote bag, honey," she said, her words breathy and labored. "If you could reach up front for it, please, and pull out my phone."

Her daughter's face crumpled in on itself as she started to cry.

"Don't worry, baby," Mallory said, alarmed by Ava's reaction. "Everything will be okay. I'll make a call and—"

And then she remembered. She didn't have her phone. Her blasted phone was back in Sugar Maple at Sticks & Strings.

Chapter 7

CHLOE

When the phone rang, we all jumped like we'd been poked by a cattle prod.

"It's not mine," Wendy said, glancing down at her ever-present iPhone.

And it wasn't the landline or my less-than-reliable smartphone.

We both glanced toward Elspeth who gave us a look that could have withered a redwood tree.

"Foolishness," she said as the mystery phone continued to ring.

"Oh, crap!" I jumped up and dashed into the hallway where I had left my tote bags filled with leftover snacks from the workshop.

I had totally forgotten about Mallory and her phone. The drive home had been such a nail biter that her problem had dropped to the bottom of my To Worry About list.

By the time I dug her phone out from beneath a dozen plastic bags filled with apple slices and cheese, it had stopped ringing.

"I bet that was Mallory," I said, sitting back down at the kitchen table. "She probably left a voicemail."

"Ava's mom?"

I nodded. Wendy's memory for names and faces always amazed me.

"What are you doing with her phone?" Wendy asked.

"She was charging it during the workshop and left it behind."

Wendy feigned a shiver. "I wouldn't want to be on the road tonight without a phone."

"Tell me about it," I said. "I hope she stopped and bought another one before she got on the highway."

"Is it unlocked?"

I nodded.

"Why don't you check and see if she left a message?"

I hesitated. It felt like an invasion of privacy and I said as much to Wendy. "Besides, wouldn't she text?"

"Who knows what she'd do," Wendy said. "It's worth a shot."

I futzed around with the phone, tapping various icons, until I reached her voicemail.

Well, almost reached it.

Please enter your password, followed by the pound sign.

So much for listening to her voicemails.

Reluctantly I clicked the text message icon and blushed when I saw a message from her husband.

"Nope," I said, "nothing for me here." I turned the phone face down on the table to both Wendy's and Elspeth's amusement.

Laria, however, had grown quiet. Her normally cheery expression had been replaced by a look of concern. I know that sounds crazy. I mean, what does a ten-month-old baby with a full belly and a dry diaper have to be concerned about but the look on her face spoke for itself.

"Does the baby look sad to you?" I asked, tickling a tiny foot with my finger.

Laria barely registered the touch.

"The wee one had a busy day," Elspeth said. "She be needing her sleep."

"She looks like she has the weight of the world on her shoulders," Wendy observed.

Laria's head drooped, her plump chin resting on her chest. Maybe Elspeth was right and I should take her to her room and tuck her in for the night.

"What's this?" I pointed toward her tightly closed right fist. A shot of hot pink peeked through.

"Some little crochet doodad," Wendy said with a shrug. "She had it with her on the way home."

I gently pried the baby's tiny fingers open so I could see what she was clutching.

"Ava's hair thingie," I said. "I guess Mallory will be coming back for more than her phone."

Clearly Laria was tired. She looked like she was half-asleep but I had the feeling she was alert and aware of everything that was going on around her.

She made a small sound, almost a whimper, and moved her hands across the tray of her highchair as if she were drawing a picture on the bright yellow plastic surface with here fingertips.

If there was one thing I had learned in my months of magickal motherhood, it was that nothing was exactly as it seemed. Not when your daughter's powers are stronger than yours and even more unpredictable.

"I think she's trying to tell us something." I pulled a few pieces of paper and a handful of markers from our junk drawer.

Wendy lifted a brow. "Isn't she a little young for that?"

"We'll find out," I said as a protective Elspeth watched closely.

I put the paper on the tray in front of Laria and placed the markers, caps off, next to them.

"She's not paying any attention," Wendy said.

"Sleep be what she needs," Elspeth chimed in. "Not play."

But I knew my daughter better than either one of them.

I waited.

Laria looked at the paper and then at the markers. She reached out with her left hand and wrapped her tiny fist around the red marker then looked up at me.

I nodded. "Go ahead, Laria," I said. "See what you can do."

I could almost feel Wendy's eyes roll back into her head.

Hand-eye coordination wasn't exactly my daughter's strong suit yet but what she lacked in fine motor skills, she made up for in sheer determination.

One oblique line from top left toward bottom right. A squiggle near the mid-point. A few wonky circles scattered about.

"Wow!" Wendy applauded Laria's efforts with enthusiasm. "I'm seriously impressed. I didn't think a ten-month-old baby could even hold a crayon."

"Neither did I," I admitted, "but we both know our girl isn't exactly your ordinary baby."

"No argument there," Wendy said with a laugh. She had witnessed Laria's first foray into flying and still couldn't quite believe it had happened.

Laria quickly filled the page with scribbles then reached for a clean sheet. That alone was pretty darned amazing.

I think that was when I realized she wasn't just making random doodles on the page. She might be trying to tell us something.

We watched as she put down the red marker and picked up a green one. She inspected the tip for a moment, then exchanged it for a blue marker. Her movements were clumsy but deliberate. She held the broad tip of the blue marker against the snowy white piece of paper and giggled as a blue blot spread outward from the point. I heard her draw in a deep breath as she began moving the marker across the page in a series of crisscrossed lines that made absolutely no sense to me.

I was so proud I could scarcely breathe. My baby was blasting her way through the developmental markers and I felt like she'd graduated Harvard *summa cum laude*. My girl's powers weren't dependent upon falling in love years down the line. Her powers were blossoming with every day that passed. Every child in Sugar Maple possessed powers humans could never imagine, but not one of them had flown like a bird long before a first birthday rolled around. She was destined for greatness.

Laria made a sound of frustration and pushed the red marker off the highchair tray. It fell to the floor and rolled under Wendy's chair. The scribbled-on piece of paper quickly followed.

"There be a price to pay for keeping the wee one up late," Elspeth said as she loaded the dishwasher.

"You're getting old and jaded, Elspeth," I teased, my eyes never leaving Laria. "You've watched so many babies grow up that you don't recognize greatness when you see it."

The ancient troll harrumphed. I'd never actually heard a harrumph before, but it was unmistakable.

"The babe be special," she admitted, a tiny smile twitching the corners of her mouth, "but a sleeping babe be better."

Of course I ignored her. There was no way I was going to stop Laria's exploration for something as mundane as sleep.

Muttering something about foolish new mothers, Elspeth took her leave. As a rule, her weekends were her own. I never asked where she went or what she did when she wasn't here with us, but she had mentioned that she was to midwife a birth in a different dimension tomorrow morning. I told her I would hold a good thought for mother and child.

Wendy reached under her chair for the fallen piece of paper and the tossed marker and then put them on the kitchen table. Laria had managed to grab an orange marker with her fist and was laboriously moving it across a blank sheet of paper.

"The girl is on a mission," Wendy said. "I hope you have plenty of paper."

"Tons," I said. "We keep it around for when Luke's nieces and nephews come to visit."

"How often is that?" Wendy asked.

"Often enough," I said.

"How do you keep the baby from flying over to them?"

"Dumb luck so far," I said. "It was easy keeping Sugar Maple's secrets from the tourists, but once the tourists became family . . ." I let my words fade away.

"Like me," Wendy said, with a laugh.

"Yep," I said, laughing with her. "Exactly like you."

Laria made a grumble of clear exasperation and redoubled her efforts.

"She's definitely trying to say something." I peered down at the wonky, concentric circles she was inscribing. "I wish I knew what it was."

"Maybe she just likes making shapes," Wendy said. "This might be her artistic side stepping up."

That was something I hadn't thought of. "Could be," I said. "She was definitely interested in the knitting this afternoon." Laria had hung onto little Ava's every word and action during the impromptu needlework lesson.

But my newly minted maternal instinct told me there was something more going on here.

The question was, what?

Chapter 8

MALLORY

The only good thing Mallory could say about the pain tearing through her body was that it kept her awake. Her head felt like she'd gone in the ring with a MMA contender. The rest of her felt like she'd lost.

But at least she was awake.

Ava had found some plastic garbage bags and an old moving van blanket under a pile of books Mallory had earmarked for the library fundraiser. They were currently huddled together beneath them, but Mallory knew it wasn't close to enough. Darkness was falling quickly and the snow showed no sign of stopping. The inside of the minivan was growing colder by the minute and the chances of being rescued any time soon were slim to none.

They were in deep trouble. There was no sense pretending otherwise. She would put on a good front for her little girl's sake but without a phone to call for help, the odds were against them being found any time soon.

Her hand rested lightly on her still flat stomach. Pain of any kind wasn't a good sign. This was supposed to have been a wonderful day. First there was the knitting workshop that Ava had been looking forward to, then the trip to Rhode Island where she and Josh, thanks to the wonders of modern technology, would share the news of their pregnancy with his parents.

Josh!

He would know immediately that there was something wrong. Her spirits soared. He was probably freaking out right now, wondering why she hadn't texted him her progress. His parents would phone the police and they'd send out a search party and before you knew it, Mallory and Ava would be safe and warm.

Except that wasn't going to happen. Josh didn't know anything about Sugar Maple. All he knew was that she'd planned to take Ava to a knitting workshop on the way to Rhode Island. They'd search the highways between her upper New York State home and his parents' house near Little Compton.

They wouldn't be looking for the mother and daughter in a forgotten piece of woodlands in the middle of nowhere in Vermont.

She was grateful for the snacks Chloe and her crew had stuffed into their goodie bags. The bottles of water alone would get them through the night and into the morning. Ava munched on cheese and almonds while all Mallory could manage was a few sips of water.

"Someone will find us soon, right?" Ava was trying very hard to be brave. "Someone will come looking for us."

"Definitely," Mallory said. The sound of her own voice made her head ache even more. "I'm sure the police keep an eye out for people in trouble when there's a bad snow storm."

"Are we in trouble?" Ava's voice trembled the tiniest bit, but enough to make Mallory's heart ache.

How honest was too honest?

"We had an accident," she said carefully. "We'll need help with the car."

"You need help, too," Ava observed.

There were times when Mallory wished her little girl wasn't quite so observant.

"I'll be fine," Mallory said, trying hard to focus against the double vision plaguing her. At least the bleeding from her head wound had slowed to a trickle. "The important thing is--"

The silence in the minivan was absolute. Her words had disappeared mid-sentence.

"Mommy?" Ava's lower lip began to tremble.

"...fine," she heard herself mumble. "...no worry."

Oh God, what was happening to her? She felt herself fading in and out like a bad phone connection. She had to hang on for Ava... for the baby...for Josh...for herself. She was stronger than this. She had figured her way out of dangerous situations before, hadn't she? All they had to do was get through the night and everything would make sense in the morning. The storm would have played itself out and the road crews would be busy clearing away the snow and looking for stranded motorists.

"I can't see out the windows," Ava said, snuggling closer. "Do you think a bear might get us?"

Mallory sucked in a deep breath of cold air to clear her head. "If you can't see out, the bear can't see in."

Her daughter's small body stiffened with alarm. "But there are bears out there."

"Lots of deer," she said carefully, "but no bears."

Mallory wasn't sure Ava believed her. Of course there were bears. This was Vermont. They were in the woods. And it was too early in the year for the bear population to be tucked away for a long winter's nap.

But no mother worth her stretch marks would tell her child any of that or the fact that the bucket they used for collecting rocks on their river walks back home would have a whole different purpose tonight.

The woods might be hiding all manner of wildlife, but it also shielded them from the worst of the storm. The trees provided a natural barrier to the high winds and deflected some of the heavy snow.

But even trees had their breaking point and as the evening wore on, the occasional loud crack and ground-shaking thud reminded both of them that the sheltering woods could turn against them.

"Mommy, are you awake?"

"Sure, honey. Go to sleep. I'm keeping watch."

"Mommy, say something!" A small hand pushed against Mallory's shoulder. "I need to go."

"Okay, we'll take care of everything."

"Mommy! Why don't you answer me?"

What was wrong with her daughter? Mallory had answered every question.

Ava was crying. She could hear the small sobs.

"Don't cry, honey," she said. (Or, at least, thought she said.) "Get the bucket from the back and everything will be just fine."

She heard the sound of the door sliding open.

She felt the blast of snow swirling into the passenger compartment.

She heard the door slide shut behind her daughter.

She didn't know where her daughter was going or why.

"Ava, stop!" Was she really crying out or was it all in her head? "Come back!"

But there was nothing but the rush of wind and the sound of the snow against the windows.

Chapter 9

CHLOE

In the blink of an eye, Laria went from silent concentration to frantic wailing.

Wendy and I exchanged puzzled looks.

"Don't ask me," my childless cousin said. "I don't have a clue."

Unfortunately, neither did I.

My baby girl was sobbing as if her tiny heart were breaking and nothing I said or did was good enough to calm her down.

The thing is, my daughter isn't one of those babies who cry all the time. Oh sure, there is the occasional wail of frustration, the grumble when her diaper change doesn't come around fast enough, but for the most part she made her needs well known without eardrum-shattering sobs.

So you can imagine how shocked I was when she launched into a downright operatic display of serious displeasure over what seemed like nothing to us.

"I think that's what they call a tantrum," Wendy said, wincing as Laria hit one of those notes they claim only dogs can hear.

"I think you're right."

The Terrible Twos were going to require noise-cancelling headphones if this was any indication.

I tried talking to Laria, but she ignored me. Her fingers were curled into tight little fists. Her face was crunched into a gargoyle-like mask. Tears splashed unchecked down her chubby cheeks. Her legs thrashed against the seat of the high chair. It was a whole-body assault that made me wonder if I would ever really understand my own child.

Wendy was wide-eyed. "Maybe she wants to be picked up," she suggested, then held her hands up, palms outward. "Not that I'm volunteering, you understand."

I scooped the baby from the high chair, amazed by the power behind those tiny arms and legs.

"Does something hurt?" I asked my wailing child. "Your diaper is dry. I know you ate. What's wrong?" I cringed at the pleading tone of my voice, but I was getting desperate. "What are you trying to say?"

"I think she was talking to me."

I practically leaped out of my skin when Gavan manifested in the middle of my kitchen in all his alpha male glory. He was built like a linebacker but in Gavan's case it wasn't a product of superhero padding. He had that not-quite-of-this-world aura that made his beautifully embroidered cloak seem like a fashion choice even GQ would embrace. The women of Sugar Maple had been whispering about him from the day he introduced himself and it was no wonder my human cousin Wendy had fallen under his spell.

But it was the fact that he had fallen under Wendy's spell that had everyone talking.

Laria's wailing stopped cold and she favored him with a look of serious satisfaction.

Wendy glowed.

I just wanted to know what the heck was going on.

"What do you mean, the baby was talking to you?"

He spread his enormous hands wide. "I have no explanation. She called to me and I am here."

"How exactly did she call to you?" I asked, even though I was beginning to put it together.

He struggled for a moment, clearly searching for a common thread. "In Sugar Maple, you communicate with blueflame. Laria reached out to me using the earliest form."

"You're saying she used old magick."

"Her magick is ancient and very powerful," he said, "and will continue to be powerful far into the future."

Which was his way of saying magick was magick and I'd better get on board with that fact because my daughter was way ahead of the rest of us.

He extended his massive arms toward Laria. I hesitated. Not because I feared he would harm her in any way, but because I still wasn't sure what was happening or why.

Laria made up my mind for me. Her entire body reached out to him and I handed my daughter over to the man my parents had betrothed me to all those years ago and waited to see what would happen next.

Naturally that was when Mallory's cell phone chirped.

Wendy was sitting closest to it and she pounced, answering it before the second ring.

"Mallory's phone," she said, flipping it to speaker. "This is Wendy."

Silence. The crackle and pop of a glitchy connection was followed by the flat sound of a non-existent one.

"A hang-up," Wendy said with a shrug, as she handed it to me.

I wasn't so sure.

"You two stay here." I remembered what Luke had said about the old magick possibly causing electrical interference. "I'm taking the cell into the back bedroom."

If Gavan's magick really was doing something to block reception, maybe a little distance would help.

I had barely stepped into the bedroom, when the phone rang again.

"Mallory's phone," I said. "This is Chloe speaking."

"Can I speak to Mallory?" The voice was deep, male, and concerned.

"Who is this?" I asked.

"This is her husband. Why are you answering my wife's phone?"

"I'm Chloe Hobbs," I said. "Mallory and Ava attended a knitting workshop at my yarn store today. It started to snow pretty hard so we ended early. I'm afraid she left her phone behind."

Another long silence.

"Hello?"

More tinny, scratchy sounds from the phone. "I'm here," he said. "I'm her husband, Josh. She was supposed to call me."

"She's probably waiting out the blizzard," I said, with more assurance than I was actually feeling. "I'm sure she'll call you once she gets settled somewhere. Pay phones don't exist any more. She'll have to find a room first."

"Where exactly are you? She was on her way to my parents' place in Rhode Island."

"Vermont," I said. "I know she was headed for the highway."

Gavan peered into the room with Laria happily tucked into the crook of his right arm, and the connection went flat, emitting the weird dead air sensation that cellphones specialize in. I waved him away and the connection crackled back into existence.

"Give me your number," I said, "and I'll call you back from a landline."

I thanked the universe that Luke required a working old school landline for his job.

"I can't give you a number. I'm in Afghanistan," he said. "I'll give you my folks' number in Rhode Island. You give me your landline. We'll work this out."

We exchanged numbers. I threw in my cell for good measure.

"I don't like this," he said. "Mallory's a great winter driver but she's pregnant and—"

I felt the blood rush from my head. "She's pregnant?"

"Early days," he said. "We were going to tell my folks this weekend."

I scrambled for something to say that would ease his mind. "The

64

motels along the highway are probably filling up super fast. It might take awhile for her and Ava to get settled."

"She's a great driver," he said again, "and they've probably lowered the speed limits to a crawl."

"I'm sure that's it," I agreed.

"I'll give the folks a call. Maybe Mallory checked in with them."

"Great idea," I said. "My husband's the police chief here in town and he says—"

The connection was cut off.

I hurried back into the kitchen, followed by Gavan and Laria. My mind was sparking with possibilities.

I looked at Laria who was looking back at me from her spot in Gavan's arms. Ava's crocheted flower peeked out from her right fist in a flash of hot pink.

I finally knew what she was trying to tell us.

"You're worried about Ava and her mom, aren't you?" I asked my daughter.

I didn't expect an answer but then again, you never know. I hadn't expected my baby girl to fly around town under her own power either and she's already done that three times.

Laria's steady gaze met and held mine. I waited for some kind of communication, verbal or magickal, between us, but there was nothing.

"You're right," Gavan said. "Laria is very worried. She knows they are lost and in danger."

Okay, now it was getting seriously weird, even for Sugar Maple.

"How did she tell you that?" I demanded. "As far as I know, we're still waiting for her first word."

Wendy's eyes darted from Laria to Gavan to me, like we were all center court at Wimbledon.

"Her magick is like our own." He offered me one of his devastating smiles. "Her skills are impressive. You have much to be proud of, Chloe. Your daughter will one day be the most powerful of all."

I couldn't deal with his prediction at the moment. Sometimes the thought of my daughter's future scared the daylights out of me.

"So where are they? Rhode Island? New Hampshire? On the

highway some place?" I could hear the hysteria building in my voice but couldn't control it. "You can't tell half a story."

"That is all I know," he said.

"Do you have more to say?" I asked my daughter. "Please, Laria, if you know where they are, help us find them."

She started to cry again, big gulping sobs that overpowered her tiny body. I reached for her, but she clung tighter to Gavan, her baby fingers tracing patterns against the broad expanse of his chest.

Patterns, I realized, not aimless scribbles. Lines bisecting lines, overlapping circles traced across the intricate embroideries on his magnificent cloak.

I grabbed the pages she had marked up and shoved them toward Gavan. "This is what she's been trying to tell us," I said, driven by some crazy kind of maternal logic. "I think she's drawing a map to guide us to Mallory and Ava."

"There's no orientation," Wendy said, shaking her head. "No landmarks. No nothing. She might be trying to draw a map but it just doesn't translate into anything we can understand."

"You're wrong." Gavan's sonorous voice filled the room. He transferred into the crook of his arm and spread the pages on the table before him. "She's telling us to look in the woods."

I stared down at the marks on the pages. I might as well have been looking at the Dead Sea Scrolls. "I don't see anything."

Wendy squinted at the array of drawings. "I don't see anything either."

"That is because this is in the graphic language of Rohesia's fore-bears and beyond." He explained how his early ancestors passed down their stories through curves and angles instead of words. After they made the change to an oral tradition, the curves and angles morphed into a method of mapping their homeland. "We were not an open society," he said, a bemused expression on his face, "but we drew others to us with a road map as precise as those talking devices in your cars."

Wendy leaned forward. "GPS."

I was growing impatient. "So where are Mallory and Ava?"

"I do not know."

I wanted to wrap my hands around his pretty neck and squeeze, but I restrained myself. "I thought you said this was some kind of wonder map that would lead us right to them."

"I said that Laria is attempting to draw a map that will accomplish that. I do not know the terrain well enough yet to interpret the clues."

Wendy looked at me. "You've lived here all your life. If anyone knows the geography, you do."

"I can chart a three-hundred-stitch, twenty-row lace pattern, but I can barely read a map," I said. "And besides, Gavan said that Laria is giving us old school markings."

Which brought us back to where we started. I asked Gavan to interpret what he was looking at in the hope that something might click. Laria struggled for a better view.

"There is no storm in this rendering," Gavan said. "It represents a different season of the earth."

"Go on," I said as Laria watched and listened.

"There are mountains surrounding the area." He pointed toward a blob in the upper left-hand corner of the top page. "And trees."

"This is Vermont," I said, not as kindly as I should have. "Of course there are trees."

Wendy shot me a look. I ignored it.

"Where do you see trees?" she asked him as the baby moved restlessly in his arms.

He pointed toward blank spaces scattered thickly on the page. "Some pine. Some maple. Each grove exists separately."

I nodded. That was pretty much the way our woodlands broke down. "What else?"

"A darkness that could be a cave. Streams of water."

I instantly thought of the waterfall that had served as a portal to different dimensions and a source of power for the Fae. "Streams like a waterfall?"

"It is unclear, but I do not think so."

Laria was growing agitated, pulling away from Gavan as she

reached down for the papers she had drawn on. She still clutched Ava's crocheted flower in her right hand.

"That could be anywhere," I said as my daughter made noises clearly meant to convey baby exasperation. "I don't see anything that would say this is near Sugar Maple. Trees. Water. I mean, come on."

"That's the problem," Wendy said. "It doesn't have to be anywhere near here. For all we know, Mallory and Ava are in New Hampshire or Massachusetts or even Rhode Island by now."

It was anybody's guess.

"I'm going to phone her in-laws," I said. "Maybe we're worried over nothing. She and Ava might be sitting in front of a roaring fire, sipping hot cocoa right this minute."

I grabbed the trusty landline and punched in the number Josh had given me.

"We haven't heard from Mallory," her mother-in-law said after I identified myself. "We're very worried."

We discussed the blizzard and the number of roads, both big and small, which had been closed down for the duration.

"Josh thinks we should call the police and file a missing persons report," his mother said, "but with the storm and all, I told him we should wait a bit."

"My husband is the chief of police here in Sugar Maple," I offered. "You have my word that he will do whatever he can to locate Mallory and Ava and make sure they're safe."

"Your husband is the chief of police? I'd like to speak with him."

"I'm afraid the storm has him stranded in Philadelphia," I said, "but I'll call him and tell him about the situation."

"And he can ask his patrolmen to search for Mallory and Ava, right?"

She sounded so hopeful that I didn't have the heart to tell her that Luke was not only the chief of the Sugar Maple police force, he was the *entire* Sugar Maple police force. "I'll phone him as soon as we hang up."

"We promised Josh that we would contact the highway police if they didn't show up by eight o'clock."

"It's not quite six o'clock," I said. "I'm sure we'll know something by eight."

"Please do whatever you can," Mallory's mother-in-law said, her voice betraying her fear. "They're our only family."

"Don't worry," I said. "We'll find them."

At least, I hoped we would.

Chapter 10

MALLORY

Mallory floated in and out of consciousness, unsure how much time had passed since Ava left.

But had she really left? Mallory wasn't sure. Maybe she had imagined her daughter climbing out of the minivan and disappearing into the storm. Her mind was all hazy and jumbled; her vision doubled like a funhouse mirror. She patted the seat next to her, hoping to find a sleeping Ava curled up next to her under the makeshift blankets.

But she was alone.

She hadn't imagined the sound of the door sliding shut. Ava was really gone.

Without her phone she had no idea what time it was. She berated herself for abandoning her trusty old school watch. How long had her daughter been gone? She hadn't a clue. Five minutes? An hour? A day? Panic exploded inside her chest, exaccrbating the mind-numbing pain.

It didn't matter how long Ava had been gone. It was already too long.

She had to find her.

The simple act of sliding open the door sent sharp bursts of pain through her head and chest and belly. She ignored it and pushed forward, tumbling from the minivan and landing on her knees in a soft mountain of snow.

"Ava!" she called, praying her voice carried. "Ava!"

She sounded tiny in the vastness of the storm. It would be a miracle if her daughter could hear her over the screaming wind.

Freshly fallen snow had obliterated her daughter's footsteps. She struggled to think the way Ava would think but her own thoughts were messy and disjointed, circling around like a hamster on a wheel.

Her sense of direction was usually on point but not today. She was so dizzy that it was hard to stay on her feet. She needed to get back to the minivan and regain her bearings.

She needed a plan.

The car seemed so far away. She hadn't taken more than a few steps in any one direction but now she had miles to go. How had that happened? She felt as if she were trapped on one of those amusement park rides where you can't tell up from down.

She slipped twice, falling to the ground in a graceless sprawl. Distantly she noted streaks of blood on the white snow. Blood wasn't good. She knew that. Blood meant trouble. But she was so tired and the pain kept slamming against her like an invisible battering ram.

Ava. Her daughter's name repeated over and over in her head.

Ava.

Ava.

No matter how hard she tried, how loudly she called her daughter's name, only the wind answered.

She was so tired. So cold. The snow beneath her feet was soft and inviting.

The lure of sleep, deep and dreamless sleep, was irresistible.

Maybe if she rested for just a minute, she would somehow figure out what to do.

Chapter 11

CHLOE

I hung up from my call to Mallory's in-laws feeling worse than I had before. While I hadn't exactly lied, the truth rested somewhere between what I said to them and what I meant. More than anything, I wanted to be able to find Mallory and Ava and get them back on their way to Rhode Island. Whether or not I would be able to accomplish that was anybody's guess.

It seemed that my baby daughter might hold the key to locating Mallory and Ava but despite how much I loved her, I didn't understand her one single bit.

I might have more than my share of magickal powers, but I don't have ESP, and that was exactly what I needed right now. My powers hadn't showed up until I was thirty and in love for the first and only time. Laria's powers blossomed with her first breath and continued to grow.

Right now she was scaring the daylights out of me. Her cries grew louder by the second, heartbreaking wails that seemed to come from the center of her baby soul. Gavan tried to forge a link with her, some kind of connection that might help us understand what was going on, but so far, he wasn't having any luck at all.

I'm not proud of this fact, but in a way, I was relieved. The thought that he might forge a deeper connection with my child than I was capable of doing made my mommy insecurities ratchet up a few thousand notches.

The realization struck me that it was all guesswork. We assumed her scribbles were maps. We thought she was worried about Ava and Mallory. We guessed that the crying was out of frustration that we just couldn't seem to understand.

Then again, maybe she was campaigning for her next bowl of spaghetti with broccoli and butter and we were barking mad for thinking otherwise.

Let's face it: we didn't know anything. All we had were a fistful of papers, a cranky baby, and a lot of guesswork.

Still, it was better than nothing. This feeling of helplessness was more than I could handle. I'd rather do something, anything, than just stand by waiting for someone else to jump in.

Wendy made us a pot of tea, while Gavan stood by the back door, taking in everything with that all-encompassing (and slightly unnerving) gaze of his.

"You have imps," he said.

"We haven't seen imps around here in years." The last infestation had occurred when I was a baby, far too young to remember. Everything I knew about them came from stories I'd heard growing up. Imps were like humanoid Corgis, yappy and argumentative and likely to bite you in the ankle.

"They left their mark near the nursery window," he said. "It is to be expected. They always guard the children of the leader."

"I would rather have an infestation of army ants," I said.

Gavan laughed. The sound surprised all of us. "They are powerful protectors," he said. "Their presence is a good thing."

"If they can calm Laria down, bring on the imps," I muttered.

"I didn't know someone so small could make so much noise," Wendy observed.

"I'm going to call Luke," I said as I tried to think. "Maybe he can help us figure this out."

Wendy brightened. "He's a cop. He must know all about maps and landmarks and all that stuff."

"How will he see the maps?" Gavan asked. "He has no powers of his own."

"He doesn't need powers," I said. "I'll take a picture with my phone and send it to him."

"I do not understand how that is possible."

"Stay tuned," I said, feeling encouraged for the first time in hours.

At the very least, maybe the sound of his voice would soothe his baby girl.

I snapped a few pictures then tried to call Luke from my cell but couldn't hang on to a connection long enough to send them. Frustrated, I switched to the old cordless handset from the landline. I whispered a thank-you to Luke for keeping it charged up.

He answered his cell on the second ring.

"Where are you?" I asked in lieu of hello.

"The airport hotel," he said, sounding puzzled. "Why?"

"I need your help."

"Tell me," he said, snapping instantly into cop mode.

I laid out the situation as quickly and clearly as I could. "We think it's some kind of map of a wooded area, but none of us can figure out where the exact area is."

There was a long silence. "And you're saying our ten-month-old daughter drew it."

"That's exactly what I'm saying."

"Our baby daughter who can't handle a spoon yet."

"Luke, I know it sounds crazy but trust me, she drew it."

"Did you ask her to explain?"

"You know she can't talk."

"Hey, she's an aviator and a cartographer. Talking should be a piece of cake."

"We can banter later. I need your help now. Mallory's in-laws are going to call the highway patrols between here and Rhode Island if I don't come up with something fast."

"If they're stuck on the highway, they'll be found without a phone call," he said. "Once the plows are out, they'll be checking for stalled cars, fender benders, getting travelers to shelter."

"What about before the plows?"

"Before the plows, nobody's going anywhere."

"They're giving me until eight o'clock."

"So what if they call the staties," Luke said. "They have resources we don't."

"And we have secrets they couldn't imagine." I sucked in a deep breath. "Think about it, Luke. If they start crawling all over Sugar Maple, we'll be found out in two seconds."

"That's not going to happen."

"How do you know?"

"State police patrol state roads and highways. Sugar Maple is out of their jurisdiction."

"And what if they can't find Mallory and Ava? What then?"

"We'll deal with that problem when and if we get there."

Somehow I didn't find that very reassuring.

"The map is pretty crude," I warned him as I wandered through the house, with Gavan and Wendy trailing close behind, hoping to bump into a hot spot. "It probably won't make any sense, but I need your opinion. Gavan thinks she's communicating in some old magick type of pictographs."

"Like the drawings in front of a rest room that differentiate between males and females."

"Except not half as easy to interpret."

Luke's silence spoke volumes. He wasn't buying any of it.

"Forget you're a logical, real world cop for a minute," I said. "Think Sugar Maple."

"This is a lot even for Sugar Maple."

"Don't cops follow every lead, no matter how implausible?"

"Not if it means tracking footsteps on the moon."

"Humor me," I said. "I think this means something." My human intuition was working overtime.

Another long silence then, "Okay, don't waste time waiting for cell service. Fax it over to me at the hotel." He read the fax number off his welcome packet and I repeated it back to him.

We hung up and I tore through the house in search of our ancient fax machine. I finally found it under the bed, squeezed in between two big blanket bags filled with scraps of unidentified yarn.

"Don't say a word," I warned Wendy as I wiped off a thick layer of dust. "I forgot to tell the house sprites to clean under the furniture."

Wendy made a noise somewhere between a snort and a flat-out laugh. "Nobody needs to tell me to dust. I'd be out of business if I did such a terrible job."

"Maybe you should move to Sugar Maple," I said as I carried the fax machine into the kitchen and attached everything that needed attaching. "Give the house sprites a little competition."

She and Gavan exchanged a look that I pretended I didn't see.

It took me a moment to remember how to work the fax but the machine rumbled to life, dialed out, and did its thing.

"Okay," I said, stepping back from the fax. "Any time, Luke."

"The maps are still here," Gavan said, "but Luke sees them. What brand of magick is this that links to humans and their machines?"

"It's called technology," I said with a rueful grin, "and it just might put us magicks out of business one day."

He looked overwhelmed and I felt a tug of sympathy for him. The man possessed powerful magick, but everyday life in the twenty-first century continued to overwhelm him. I could only imagine how difficult it was for the rest of Rohesia's clan. Maybe I hadn't done them any favors when I welcomed them to Sugar Maple.

But right now I had other things to worry about.

"What's taking him so long?" Wendy fumed, pacing the length of my small kitchen. "Why doesn't he get back to us?"

Ten minutes went by.

Then twenty.

We were coming up on an hour since I sent the pages to him

and I was starting to wonder if maybe I should send them out again when the fax buzzed to life, spilling new pages onto the floor.

Moments later, the phone rang. I grabbed again for the cordless.

Luke didn't bother with hello. "Grab the pages and follow along," he said, in full-out cop mode.

I spread them out on the table. We all gathered around. Even Laria seemed focused.

"Ready," I said. "I'm putting you on speaker."

"I can read individual stands of trees and the basic terrain, but I can't pinpoint the location. The problem is that a hell of a lot of New England reads exactly like this."

I managed not to groan.

"It's an aerial view, so it has to be Sugar Maple," he continued.

"An aerial view?" That surprised me. "Are you sure?"

"Positive." He explained something about foliage density and the way Gavan had interpreted streams, ponds, and creeks. "I used Google Maps to verify that I was on the right track."

"And you believe it is Sugar Maple."

"It has to be," he said. "Sugar Maple is the only town Laria has flown over."

"Give her time," I said as she squirmed against my shoulder.

His laugh was low and amused. For a moment, daddy trumped cop.

"It's still a long shot," he said. "This is all speculation."

"I know that," I said, "but Laria is trying very hard to tell us something and we have to follow through. The problem is, we don't know where to start."

"I started with some basic deductive reasoning to narrow the search area," Luke said. "We know they didn't go south of Sugar Maple because the highway is northwest."

We all nodded, which was kind of silly since we weren't using FaceTime.

"If they made it to a motel that was anywhere near the highway, they would have phoned Josh's parents in Rhode Island. Since we know they didn't call, we can rule that possibility out for now."

This was Luke at his best and, despite the high stakes involved, I loved listening to him lay out the facts.

"So let's assume they turned back before getting on the highway," he went on. "That places them north of us."

"Laria flew over the woods to the north," I said.

"More than once," Luke said. "Which means there are two possibilities: either Laria is telling us flat out that Mallory and Ava are stranded in the woods north of Sugar Maple or she's extrapolating her first-hand knowledge to convey some place else."

"In other words," Wendy said, a slight edge to her voice, "you don't have a clue."

"I have plenty of clues," he shot back. "What I don't have are facts."

"Given what we know"-- I paused for a moment to aim a little side-eye Wendy's way "—or don't know for sure, what would you do, Luke?"

"I'd get out there and start looking. If they're stranded on the highway, they'll be found, no problem. But local road crews won't start operating until the snowfall ends. If they got stuck on one of the side roads, we can get to them a lot quicker, especially if you add a little magick to the mix."

Gavan would begin to the northwest, heading toward the state road that led to the highway. Wendy would head northeast in case Mallory and Ava had turned back and somehow missed the turnoff to Sugar Maple and headed into the woods.

"The three of you need to stay in constant contact." From the tone of his voice, I knew this was not up for debate. "You don't want to put together a search party for a member of another search party."

"I understand."

"Want me to call Paul Griggs and Lorcan Meany and some of the others? I'm sure they'd come out and help."

"No!" The word burst out on its own. "I mean, thanks, but we can handle this."

"That was fast," he said. "Is there something you're not telling me?"

Of course there was. But I still hadn't come close to processing the fact that old friends and neighbors were turning against me. "There is, but we'll talk when you get home," I said. "Right now, we need to concentrate on finding Mallory and Ava."

I wasn't looking forward to telling him that his best friends in town might be working against us, but I would worry about that later.

The annotated pages, complete with Luke's own graphic interpretation of Laria's drawings, definitely helped to pinpoint the search area we would be dealing with. It didn't hurt that there was only one road in and out of Sugar Maple, but old logging trails still cut through the woods and it was possible, although unlikely, that they might have veered off onto one.

Assuming they were anywhere near Sugar Maple at all.

The whole search was probably an exercise in futility but the thought of doing nothing at all didn't sit well with any of us, and especially not with Laria. I had returned her to her high chair, which wasn't a popular decision until I gave her a new stack of blank pages and her multicolored markers. She inspected them carefully for a long moment, then pushed the pages off the tray and watched them drift down to the floor. The markers followed immediately after.

"I wish you could tell me what you're thinking," I said, crouching down so I could look into her beautiful gold eyes. "You're so far ahead of me, honey, that I don't think I'll ever catch up."

She caught and held my gaze. The air around us seemed to coalesce into a shimmering curtain of energy. Wendy and Gavan faded away. My cozy kitchen became nothing but a hazy memory.

The play of emotions on my daughter's tiny face took my breath away. She still clutched Ava's hot pink scrunchie in her fist, holding it out toward me, a look of near desperation in her eyes.

"Tell me," I whispered. "Tell me what you want us to do."

But despite the magick at her command, she was still a baby, without words to command.

"You don't need language," I urged her. "I'm listening."

An image, hazy and indistinct, took shape between us. A little girl with blond hair . . . another body lying in a clearing near a fallen tree . . . oh God, was it Ava and Mallory?

The images disappeared before I could be sure.

"Please, Laria," I begged my daughter, "bring the pictures back. I need to know where they are so we can help them."

But the effort to conjure up the images had exhausted my daughter and she fell deeply asleep, her chin resting against her chest.

"What the hell was that all about?" Wendy demanded as the room swam back into focus. "One second you were normal and the next you were zoning out. I'm not ashamed to say you scared the daylights out of me."

"It was Laria," Gavan said, "using the ways of my people to help us."

I spun around to face him. "You saw it, too?"

"No," he said, "but the energies were strong and familiar. I understood what was happening."

"They're in trouble," I said. "If what I saw is correct, the two of them are out near the edge of the woods."

"Can you pinpoint which side of town?"

I shook my head. Unfortunately Sugar Maple was surrounded by thick, dense woods that extended in every direction. "I couldn't make out any landmarks."

We were wasting time. Seeing the little girl in distress set a fire under me to stop talking and start finally doing something. Before I became a mother, I would have been first in line to search for Mallory and Ava. Maybe if Elspeth had been around I might have pulled on my snow shoes and headed out, but she wasn't. My priorities had changed and protecting Laria was now at the top of the list and always would be.

"I know this is asking a lot, but I need you two to go out there and start searching for them."

Gavan didn't hesitate. He was all in. Wendy followed but I could see that she was apprehensive.

I didn't blame her one bit.

"If Elspeth were here, I'd be out there with you." I hoped it didn't sound as lame as I was afraid it did.

Nobody said anything.

"Luke might call again," I stumbled on. "Or the in-laws. I need to man the phones."

"I know that," Wendy said gently. "You don't have to apologize for being a mom."

Was that what I was doing? I hoped not.

I ran to the back closet where we stored our winter gear and pulled out everything I could find. Wendy started layering on my sweaters, scarves, thick socks, and gloves. She topped off her ensemble with my huge ankle-length down coat, mittens, boots, and snowshoes.

I offered Luke's heaviest coat and work boots to Gavan, who said thanks, but no thanks.

"You can't go searching the woods during a blizzard dressed like that," I protested. Granted, he looked totally gorgeous in his embroidered cloak but there was no way a thin layer of embellished wool could protect him against a major storm.

"I will be fine."

"Please, Gavan," I said while Wendy watched and listened. "There's a blizzard out there. Luke's a little shorter than you are, but I think the coat will fit."

"I have been through storms before and will be again."

"You really should bundle up." I'm not sure why I couldn't let the issue go but I was like a dog with a particularly juicy bone. Maybe I just wanted him to look more like the rest of us and less . . . spectacular.

"He's magick," Wendy said, as if I needed reminding. "Weather doesn't bother him."

"Magick doesn't protect you against everything this world can throw at you," I said, sounding very much like a mom. "You still have to be careful."

Gavan met my eyes. It wasn't difficult to know exactly what he was thinking. Sugar Maple wasn't the safe haven it used to be and he and Wendy were part of the reason why. We had lived in plain sight for centuries in peaceful anonymity. But now, with the addition of another human and a clan of old magicks, the balance had shifted toward suspicion. And with suspicion, came danger.

It had started small. Punctured tires. Smashed windows. Foolish pranks that weren't pranks at all, but warnings. For the first time I wondered if maybe Mallory and Ava had fallen prey to one of them. I pushed the thought aside. First we had to find the mother and daughter, and then we could figure out how it all came down.

But now I was asking Wendy to go out into a blizzard and do my job for me. I was asking her to risk an encounter with beings, whether Sugar Maple residents or Rohesia's clan members, who regarded her as a danger to their existence.

I was asking her to do my job.

And that was how I ended up giving my cousin a touch of magick to see her through.

Chapter 12

WENDY

At first, I didn't feel any different. I guess that was what surprised me the most. If this was being magick, it felt a lot like being human. Talk about a disappointment.

Where was the superhero burst of strength? I was pretty sure I couldn't leap tall buildings at a single bound or shoot indestructible webs from my wrists or do any of the extremely cool things movie magicks were able to do. I also couldn't fly over the snow-covered landscape of Sugar Maple like my baby cousin Laria managed so effortlessly.

Mostly I was the same Wendy Aubry Lattimer I had been before Chloe summoned up her Book of Spells and performed a literal smoke-and-mirrors routine meant to bring me up to speed for the duration. The Book was invisible to me but the disruption in the air around me was tangible. I was impressed and maybe just a little bit terrified as I felt a burst of energy vibrate against my skin.

"It's a protective shield," Chloe said as the glittering dust and smoke settled then disappeared. "Physical harm can't touch you."

"What about magickal harm?"

"You'll be protected from the elements. You won't feel the cold."

"So I can ditch the Sasquatch jacket and hat?"

"You're still only human," Chloe said. "Better safe than sorry."

"What about magickal harm?" I asked for the second time. "You didn't answer the question."

"You'll be safe from all forms of magick within my range. Gavan will see to the rest."

She might as well have been talking to one of the cats for all that was getting through my rising fear.

Gavan took my hand and before I could register his touch, we were sucked into a swirling vortex of light and sound that made me feel like I was about to fly apart into a thousand pieces. It wasn't pain, not exactly, but it wasn't a ride on the spinning teacups either and when it was over I didn't know whether to laugh with relief or throw up on my snow shoes.

"I should have warned you," Gavan said, still holding my hand.

The world snapped back into place and I realized we were standing at the edge of the woods.

I couldn't say anything. I was shaking too hard.

"You're cold," he said.

I shook my head. Dizzy. Shocked. Disoriented. Terrified. But not cold. At least one part of the protective charm was working.

Sugar Maple was a small town, but the surrounding woods seemed like a vast and hostile place. The landscape was unforgiving and the thought of Mallory and her little girl possibly out there and in trouble was strong motivation.

Gavan moved easily across the snow like a hovercraft over a lake. I stepped forward, expecting to sink up to my knees, then gasped as I glided effortlessly toward him. He glanced over his shoulder at me and I saw the sparkle in his eyes when I caught up with him.

"Chloe didn't tell me about this!"

"She does not know of it," he said. "That is my gift to you."

Something passed between us. A moment of understanding or maybe one of sheer joy, as fragile as a soap bubble but every bit as beautiful. I hoped it would be waiting for us after we found Mallory and Ava.

The woods fanned out on either side of the narrow road that took you to the feeder road that ultimately led to the highway some twenty miles away. The silence was unnerving. The only sounds were the relentless howl of the wind and the occasional crack of a limb as it broke free of a snow-heavy tree.

The thought of being alone out there scared hell out of me. I wanted to turn and run back to Chloe's cottage and lock the door behind me. I wanted to cling to Gavan like a barnacle. The one thing I didn't want to do was strike out into the woods on my own.

Gavan went over the game plan once more. He had committed the annotated map to memory. I had a copy stashed in the pocket of Chloe's puffy coat. The plan was simple enough. He would walk to the northwest. I would walk to the northeast. If luck and magick were with us, we would find mother and daughter long before we reached the feeder road that led to the highway.

To be honest, I didn't believe they were in the woods. I would bet my yarn stash that they were sitting in an endless line of cars on the highway waiting for the plows and the sand trucks to make the road passable, but night was falling and we had to do something.

My cell phone vibrated against my hip in an eruption of snaps, crackles, and pops. I glided a fair distance from Gavan and answered Chloe's call.

"No news yet," I said. "We're just outside of town."

"Is Gavan still there?" she asked.

"Yes," I said. "I had to put a little distance between us to answer the call. We're about to split up and start the search."

"Call me," she said, sounding more than a little frantic. "If you see something or you have questions, call me. Mallory's in-laws will be getting back to me any minute, and I need to be able to tell them we're making progress."

"You do know the odds are that Mallory and Ava are safe and sound on the highway, waiting for the plows to come through."

"So I keep hearing," she said. "I wouldn't mind a little proof."

"Trust me, there is no way a car could drive through these trees." What path existed was barely wide enough for your average human.

"The old logging trails are wide enough for a minivan," she said, while Gavan waited. "You'll see them when you get closer to the feeder road."

I didn't bother asking why any sane driver would choose to leave the feeder road and plunge into the woods.

Instead, I promised to keep her up to date then ended the call.

"She's worried," I said to Gavan as I walked back toward him.

"She has reason to be," he said. "Laria's senses tell her that the child Ava is in trouble and that she is nearby. That is the reason for the drawings and the tears. It would be unwise to doubt her."

"She's ten months old. That's one reason."

"A short time in your world," he said, with a quick smile, "but long enough in mine."

"Do you think we'll find them here?" I asked.

"Laria believes it."

He didn't say "case closed" but I heard it in his words.

It unnerved me that a grown man would place so much trust in a baby's intuition, even though said baby was blessed with magickal powers I couldn't begin to understand. When I tried to envision Mallory and Ava, I saw them tucked away in their minivan, munching cookies and cheese and fruit from the goodie bags Chloe had provided and waiting in a long line of vehicles for the snow to stop. The situation would be tedious. Uncomfortable. Definitely boring. But dangerous? I didn't think so and I fully expected to be proven right before the night was over.

"How will I let you know if I find them?" I asked as we prepared to part. "Smoke signals?"

The reference was lost on him and I was reminded once again of the vast gulf that divided us.

He moved his left hand in a sweeping gesture and a glittering braided cord appeared in the space between us. One end was wrapped around his right wrist. To my surprise, the other end was looped around mine.

"We will separate but we will not be separated," he said. "This infinite chain will keep us connected."

The words were deeply romantic, although they weren't meant to be. I pushed my fantasies into the darker corners of my mind and concentrated on what he was telling me.

It all sounded good in theory. Once we parted, the chain would be invisible. The weight was undetectable. Without any help from me, it would adjust to the distance between us, however far, and yet it took just one sharp tug on the chain to bring us together again.

I guess my skepticism was showing because Gavan lifted my chin with his index finger and met my eyes.

"Trust in the magick, Wendy," he said in that molten honey voice I heard in my dreams. "Tonight you must give over to all you don't understand."

Easier said than done, I thought. I was a product of the human world, a place where magick existed only in fairy tales and the Hallmark Channel.

"You're asking a lot of me," I said, as a shiver ran up my spine. "I'm much better at trusting myself."

Somewhere in the distance we heard a loud crack as a tree limb broke off and hit the ground.

He said nothing. The moment stretched like the cord binding us together.

"It's getting dark," I said. "We'd better get started."

I pulled a Mag Lite from my pocket and switched it on. The light cut a path deep into the snow-shrouded woods. I'm not sure how he did it, but apparently Gavan had a light source all his own.

It took me a moment to accept the fact that I was walking on top of the snow and not through it. Gavan lingered in the background until I got the hang of it. When I turned to give him the okay sign, he was already gone.

Although I grew up in Maine, I wasn't what you would call an outdoorsy kind of girl. Bailey's Harbor is a small town with a lot of undeveloped forests and farmland, a popular spot for hikers and campers, but the only hiking I'd done up until now was from yarn shop to yarn shop in search of new indie dyers. My camping experience was limited to making S'mores at the kitchen stove. I'm not crazy about bugs. I don't like knowing a bear might be measuring me for his dinner plate. The closest I want to get to sleeping in a tent is watching Survivor.

But there I was, in the middle of a blizzard, striding off into the woods like I actually knew what I was doing.

What on earth was wrong with me? Why didn't I say no when Chloe asked me to help? She had magick coming out of her ears. Even better, she had lived in Sugar Maple her entire life. These woods didn't hold any surprises for her. I should have volunteered to stay with the baby and let my sorceress cousin lead the search.

I knew it was fear talking. I'm not a fan of horror movies. I'm not the girl who goes down to the basement to check out the scary noise in the middle of the night. The deeper into the woods I glided, the faster my heart pounded.

Was this how Mallory and Ava were feeling? I wanted to believe they were safe and snug in their minivan, but with every second that passed, I grew more uncertain.

An owl hooted in the distance, followed by the cracking sound of yet another tree limb falling to the ground. I pressed on, methodically checking left and right as I went, searching for any sign of the missing mother and daughter, but so far, there was nothing

The protective charm Chloe had conjured up made me impervious to the cold and wind. Gavan's gift of magick had me moving swiftly and effortlessly across the deep snow. I had no sense of how much time had passed since we'd separated to begin the search, but I had the feeling I was now closer to the feeder road than I was to our starting point, still without any sign of progress.

Then it occurred to me that the first sign of progress might be stumbling onto Mallory's car with both Mallory and Ava safely tucked inside. Logic reasoned they would be moving toward Sugar Maple, not away from it as I was, so there would be no tire tracks in the snow to follow.

I jolted forward, unsure how to ramp up my speed without losing my balance. It took a few seconds of wobbling like a baby duck, but I found the groove and held it. Searching the woods had seemed an impossible task at first, but suddenly I felt like I could search the Black Forest and still have time to take a nap.

Not that I needed a nap. Adrenaline flooded my body with energy and purpose. I kept moving, stopping only to examine a depression in the snow or a slash mark on the trunk of a mature sugar maple tree. The air smelled cold and clear. No whisper of car exhaust or, God forbid, fire.

A bone, denuded and shiny, poked through a knee-high drift to my right. It was too large to belong to a rabbit or squirrel but not large enough for a bear. Definitely not human, thank God. I tried very hard not to dwell on where or what it came from. Did the four-legged creatures of Sugar Maple have magick too? I had never stopped to think about it before now. Clearly this particular one hadn't. Then again maybe he had gone up against a creature whose magick was stronger.

Survival of the fittest apparently trumped even the strongest magick.

Somehow that didn't make me feel very confident.

I'm not proud of this but for a moment I thought about turning back. I was so far out of my comfort zone that I would need a new unit of measure to calculate the distance. I had never been alone like this before. Alone in a crowd? Many times. Alone as in the only living, breathing human being for miles? This was a first.

Except I couldn't turn back. I'd made a promise to Chloe that I would do this for her and, like it or not, I would see it through.

Besides, when you glided above the snow, you left no tracks behind. I couldn't find my way back if I wanted to.

Something howled in the not-far-enough distance and every hair on my head stood straight up. Hair-wise, I was in full Einstein mode. Too bad I wasn't half as smart as Einstein. A few extra grey cells would have come in handy right about now.

Did they have wolves in Vermont? The real kind, not the were-kind like Paul Griggs and his family. I probably should have asked before we started out. Not that it would have stopped me, but it might have been good to know what I was up against.

Magick kept me moving swiftly through the woods but I wasn't convinced I was moving in the right direction. I stopped once to take another look at the map but it didn't help. Everyone else saw signs and symbols in Laria's scribbling. Even Luke, a career cop, took it seriously enough to add his own annotations and sanction a search party.

I had tried to convince myself that I saw what everyone else saw but it was a case of The Emperor's New Clothes. I didn't see anything beyond a baby's attempt to wield a crayon.

I pushed forward once again, checking my direction against my cell phone. I was on track, heading northeast just as I'd been advised.

At least that was the plan.

Looking back, I'm not sure what caught my attention first: the realization that the snow had finally stopped or the owl hooting softly from somewhere to the east.

But was it an owl? Suddenly I wasn't so sure. The sound was too gritty, too – well, too human. There was emotion in the sound that resonated with me in a way I couldn't explain.

I stood still, holding my breath, listening hard.

I wasn't exactly an ornithologist. I had a tough time telling the call of a crow from that of a robin. For all I knew, one of the Sugar Maples had been following me and was about to spring some kind of magickal prank on the poor, unsuspecting human. Or, even worse, one of Gavan's clan had decided to take matters into his or her own hands and put a stop to our friendship.

I heard it again, low and urgent, coming from my right. Turning sharply, I headed in the direction of the sound, moving quickly between the trees. The sound grew louder as I came closer.

I was scared but it didn't stop me. The low, keening cry drew me like a magnet. I had to see this through.

A white minivan rested at the edge of the clearing, its front end jammed against a towering pine tree. The faintest smell of smoke lingered in the icy air. For a second I wondered what my car was doing there but this one didn't boast advertising scrawled across the doors. Did Mallory drive a minivan? I couldn't remember. But, let's face it, what were the odds it belonged to anybody else.

"Mallory!" My voice sounded shaky and timid. "Ava!"

No response.

The doors on the passenger side were closed tight. The windshield was cracked but intact. The front end was crumpled. The airbags had deployed. They lay like punctured balloons on the floor of the minivan. Empty goodie bags from the workshop were on the back seat, along with a half-finished bottle of water. Mallory's purse was on the floor, the top flap open.

Heart pounding, I rounded the minivan so I could check out the driver's side. Blood spatter stained the dashboard and windshield. My gut twisted as I noted pinkish streaks in the snow heading off to the left of the abandoned vehicle.

"Mallory!" I called again. "This is Wendy from Sticks and Strings."

I heard nothing but silence. I told myself they couldn't have gone far, not with that amount of blood loss. The thought wasn't as comforting as I would have liked. Cautiously I slid onto the back seat, wiggling my way around the booster seat. No way was I going to leave Mallory's purse and wallet here. Besides, there was always the chance I'd find a clue to her whereabouts. If I got really lucky, maybe I'd find a note.

The contents had spilled all over the rubber mats, and rolled under the front seat. I maneuvered myself onto the floor and started gathering up two key rings, one notepad, a fistful of promotional pens, one lip gloss, and a very well-worn copy of Elizabeth Zimmerman's Knitting Workshop. I was shoving everything back into the depths of her tote when I heard the unmistakable chirp of an automatic door lock being set.

I scrambled up from the floor. I had left the door to the driver's side back seat open, but it was definitely closed now. I knew I wasn't the one who had slid it shut but there was no doubt that somebody had done the job for me.

Heart pounding, I tried to open it but the door didn't budge.

"Okay," I muttered. "Not funny. Open up!"

Maybe I needed some kind of remote control device to make it work. I pressed every button on every key fob Mallory had, but still no luck. I thought about my friends back in Bailey's Harbor. Most of them had young kids and went to great lengths to keep those kids from danger. Car doors, in particular, came under a lot of scrutiny and I remembered a conversation about locks that were operated by the driver, not the passenger. "Great news for a kidnapper," I had said to absolutely no laughter at all.

It wasn't easy propelling myself into the front seat. Chloe's puffy coat caught on one of the seat belt latches and the sound of fabric tearing filled the cabin. This minivan might have looked like mine from the outside, but that was where the similarity ended. My vehicle was bare bones. This one had all the bells and whistles. I wasn't sure what half of the levers and buttons did but I pushed and pressed and smacked with increasing frustration.

This couldn't be happening. I mean, people get locked out of cars every day of the week, but how many get locked inside them?

I had never been claustrophobic but I have to admit I was getting an itchy feeling about being trapped in a confined space. I found myself wondering how hard it would be to kick out the windshield, and then stopped myself.

Wasn't this why Gavan had bound us together with that golden cord?

I gave it a gentle pull, followed by a no-nonsense tug. Nothing happened. What was it he had said about trusting in the magick? I was trying very hard to trust, but the magick was definitely making it difficult. He wanted me to give myself over to the situation but he might as well have asked me to fly.

Cross Gavan off the list of solutions.

I pulled out my cellphone and punched in Chloe's cell.

It went straight to voicemail.

I doubled back and punched in her landline.

I was rewarded with an angry fax squawk.

I reminded myself that this was Sugar Maple, not Bailey's Harbor. The same rules didn't apply here. This might not be a mechanical glitch at all.

This might be magick.

Well, they'd messed with the wrong woman today. Thanks to Chloe, I had magick, too, and I wasn't afraid to use it.

Too bad I didn't know how.

Chapter 13

CHLOE

"All she wants to do is sleep," I said to Luke, holding the phone against my right ear while I cradled Laria against my left shoulder. "She won't eat. She won't play. She just nuzzles in and goes deeper."

"You've waited ten months for this," he said, from his hotel room at the Philadelphia airport. "Enjoy."

"I can't. Something's not right, Luke. I just know it."

"She's had one hell of a busy day. The workshop. Hanging with Ava. Drawing maps." He paused for dramatic effect. "I'm tired just listing all of it."

"You're not hearing me. She's not connecting with anything."

"I am," he said, "and I think you're reading too much into exhaustion. She's a baby. She didn't nap today. She's tired. Put her in her crib and relax."

"You make it sound so simple," I said with exasperation.

"It can be."

Easy for him to say. He hadn't seen her over-the-top behavior.

He hadn't been there when she created those aerial maps. He hadn't watched her shift gears from near-manic to almost comatose in the blink of an eye. I knew in my gut that it was all connected to Mallory and Ava but I couldn't figure out how.

"I know what's going on," Luke said, jarring me from my thoughts. "She understands that Wendy and Gavan are out there searching the woods for Ava and her mother. She's been heard. She completed her task. Help is on its way. She can sleep."

"Is this the cop speaking or the daddy?" I asked.

"A little of both," he said.

I had to admit it made sense, but I couldn't help wondering what would happen if Wendy and Gavan failed to find the missing mother and daughter. But, as with so many things, I would worry about that later.

We talked a little more about the storm, flights out of Philly, and how much we missed each other. I hung up, feeling more alone than I had in a very long time.

I also found myself wishing Elspeth were there with me. Lately I'd had the sense she was preparing me for the time when she pierced the veil and joined all who had come before her, but I hoped that wouldn't be any time soon. I could have used some of her tart trollish wisdom tonight.

The landline rang and, heart racing, I grabbed for it before the noise woke up Laria. Maybe it was Wendy with a progress report.

"We were hoping for good news by now." Mallory's mother-in-law sounded edgy and more than a little scared.

"Our people are conducting a search right now," I said, willing myself to convey nothing but positive energy and confidence. At least one of the searchers qualified as *people*. "I promise I'll let you know as soon as I have some news to report."

"We phoned the police," she said, her voice quavering just enough for me to notice. "Local and state."

I sucked in a deep breath. This wasn't what I wanted to hear but I understood how the woman must have been feeling. "What did they say?"

"Nothing helpful." There was a note of anger in her voice. "The storm has slowed down and they'll be sending out the plows and sand trucks within the next few hours. Travelers trapped on the highways will be helped as soon as they can be reached." She sounded like she was reading from a prepared script and hating every word.

I didn't say "I told you so," but I wanted to. Every now and then Mother Nature decided to remind us who was the boss. This was one of those times.

Once again I promised to let her know the second I had any news to report.

She hung up without saying goodbye.

I wanted to be out there searching with Wendy and Gavan. Still cradling a sleeping Laria, I settled down into the rocking chair near the fireplace, and tried to visualize what was happening out there. They had been gone almost an hour but I wasn't sure how time translated to distance in this case. They could have traveled five feet or five miles. It was anybody's guess.

"Come on," I muttered under my breath. "Somebody tell me something."

The words had no sooner left my mouth than Laria's eyes shot open and she let out an ear-splitting squeak that sent the cats racing for cover. I leaped to my feet, clutching my wailing daughter, as the back wall of the cottage peeled back and an army of ginger-haired imps spilled into the kitchen on glitter-flecked clouds of cinnamon-scented fog.

The last thing I wanted was an imp infestation. I ordered them to get out but they laughed at me. Have you ever heard an imp laugh? It's worse than nails on a chalkboard. Imps are always up to no good and once they make a nest in your home, you might as well put the place up for sale.

I threatened bodily harm. I swore to call down the ancestors and turn them into crickets. Nothing worked. They laughed in my face. So did my daughter. Laria, still clutching Ava's hot pink scrunchie, clapped her hands in delight. They swarmed around us, closer and closer, not quite touching but too close for my comfort.

"Shoo!" That sounded ridiculous even to me. "Get out of here!"

I might as well have been invisible. They were yipping like crazed Chihuahuas, tumbling and somersaulting at my feet. They barely reached ankle-height and probably weighed less than a quart of milk, but for some reason they triggered an almost primitive dislike in me.

Maybe it was the fangs.

Apparently they were just the coming attractions because the second Laria stopped laughing and aimed her golden-eyed gaze in their direction, they turned blue, then green, then whiter than the snow outside, and formed two cheerleading pyramids on either side of the back wall then disappeared.

My daughter's scream echoed off the mountains that surrounded our town then took aim at my heart.

"Please, Laria, please!" I begged. "What's wrong? What are you trying to tell me?"

She didn't register the sound of my voice. Her eyes didn't meet mine. She was focused inward, to a place I'd never been, and it terrified me. I shivered as beads of cold sweat trickled down my spine. She was my daughter, my flesh and blood. We shared DNA, and yet I had a better chance of making a connection with Rohesia than I did with my own child.

"What do you want?" I begged her to tell me. "Let me help you."

But she was somewhere else. A soft keening sound escaped her lips and she lifted her head toward the ceiling, eyes wide with expectation.

I jumped as the Book of Spells dropped from the ceiling, spinning like the Mad Hatter's Tea Cups. Spangles of gold and silver, shards of ruby and sapphire, shot out in every direction, both beautiful and terrifying.

The Book of Spells was mine. I took possession of all it contained on the day I came into my magick. Our history stated the Book obeyed only one Hobbs woman per generation and this was my time. I hadn't summoned it. So what was it doing here now, revealing my family's history on its pages when I hadn't asked for its presence?

Laria went silent. I could sense her concentration growing stronger as the pages flipped slowly from the beginning of our time. An image of Aerynn flashed by, followed by images of Bronwyn and Maeve and Fiona and Aislyn and the rest of the foremothers who had shaped my destiny and hers. There was an empty page where my mother Guinevere should have been, but she had been banished forever for choosing to die with her mortal husband and leave me to the hands of fate.

My page was a work in progress.

I saw myself in a glittering mirror. The face that looked back at me was old and wrinkled but it was clearly me. A man's image, faded but true, glowed in the distance behind me. Part illusion, part truth. My stomach knotted. I knew it was Luke. He was older, far older than he was now, but still the man I had fallen in love with, the man I had married. The Book was providing me a look into my future and my blood ran cold with dread. I pushed away the thought that swept in across the landscape like a howling storm. One day I would deal with losing him to time but not now.

Laria's page had yet to be written. It was the perfect color of a priceless pearl. The only mark on its flawless surface was the glittering circle of gold that gleamed from the center of the page, drawing both her attention and mine.

She was transfixed. Once again her powers of concentration intrigued and terrified me. I brushed her cheek with a gentle index finger, hoping to draw her attention from the Book and back to me, but she didn't register my touch. She clutched Ava's hot pink scrunchie to her chest and leaned forward as her image was suddenly reflected back at her from within.

She shifted position, throwing her weight away from me, and before I realized what was happening, she broke free of my arms and sailed straight toward the Book of Spells, and the beckoning circle of gold.

I hurled myself toward her, arms outstretched, straining to grab hold of a tiny arm or leg before she disappeared into the Book's dimension, but she stayed just beyond my reach. She was a guided missile, locked in on her target, and there was nothing I could do to stop her.

But, wherever she was going, she wasn't going there without me. I was right behind her as she plunged into the Book and I stayed behind her as we were buffeted by strong interdimensional winds that were carrying us to our destination. This was a section of the Book that I had never seen before. No mind-blowing displays of magick and splendor meant to remind you of the Book's power. No celestial music. No 3D slideshows featuring Hobbs clan history.

This time it wasn't about the journey; it was about the destination. No-frills astral travel. The subway versus a private jet.

And my daughter was leading the way.

I kept as close to her as the Book would allow, never losing sight of her, never allowing the combined forces of our magick to separate us. But something was wrong. She was changing before my eyes. The chubby infant was becoming a toddler . . . a little girl . . . an adolescent in full bloom . . . a woman with her own baby growing inside her.

The last of all who came before . . . the last of Aerynn.

I didn't hear the words; I felt them inside. But they sent shock waves through my body just the same.

The adult Laria was gaining speed, putting space between us. I summoned up every drop of magick I had in me and tried to launch myself into hyperdrive. The straight path that we had been following suddenly veered left, then right, then did a 360 vertical loop that made my head spin. Images flashed by of trees and lakes and villages reminiscent of Laria's map but more intricate and detailed. Then it went dark and I was spinning through a vortex without light or sound. My skin registered a chill. Moisture beaded on my forehead. I caught the smell of wet earth and tasted salt on my lips.

I tried to call to Laria, but no sound came out.

Faster. I had to move faster. She was still within reach. I could sense her presence the way I could sense my own.

Was this how it was meant to end? I had known for months that Laria's path would be far different from my own, but I had been her mother for less than a year. I wasn't ready to let her go, no matter how gifted she might be. I wanted more time with her. I wanted her to have a life of love and joy before the responsibilities of being a descendant of Aerynn took control of her life.

Suddenly the air around me thickened like oatmeal. Moving through it took strength I was no longer sure I had. The harder I tried to speed up, the slower I moved. I was losing her. She was spinning out of my reach. If I didn't catch up with her now she would be lost to me forever.

I pushed harder, harder than I had on the day I gave birth to her in a blizzard just like this one. I called on every ounce of strength, will power, determination, and, yes, even magick available to me and crashed, screaming, through the Book and back into the human world I knew and loved where I found my baby daughter waiting for me, nestled on a bed of imps, deep inside a cave.

Chapter 14

WENDY

They make it look easy on television.

All you had to do was twitch your nose or wave your hands in the air like you were swatting flies or murmur some weird words over a crystal ball while spooky smoke wreathed your face. Bingo! Instant magick.

Maybe if you were born magick it worked that way, but for someone who had just had a little magick dumped on her, it wasn't turning out to be very helpful. Oh sure, I had been able to glide over the snow at speeds even my car couldn't manage but that was pretty much where it stopped for me.

I tried everything to unlock the doors of Mallory's minivan but no luck. I even tried kicking out a window but ended up with a sore foot instead. Trust me, if I'd had access to some eye of newt or heel of toad, I would have tried that too. Captivity wasn't a good fit for me. The snow had finally stopped, which was a relief, but it was dark out there and I was alone. Whoever or whatever had set me up like this was probably having a great laugh right about now.

Or planning his or her next step.

I wasn't crazy about that thought.

I tugged again on the cord that bound me to Gavan but once more there was no response. I'm not an expert on the workings of magick, but I had the feeling I was stuck between the old and the new that Chloe was always talking about. I phoned Chloe again, both numbers, and met the same end results. This time the calls went through but she didn't answer. The phrase "sitting duck" floated through my mind. Nobody knew where I was. Even I didn't know exactly where I was. I was unnerved to realize I could see out which meant everyone else could see in.

And pretty soon I was going to need a bathroom break.

I'm not one of those women who cry over every little thing. I got through my divorce without depleting Bailey's Harbor's supply of tissues. But I was quickly reaching my breaking point.

Once again Sugar Maple had reminded me I didn't belong there. Even with my own touch of magick, however temporary, I still didn't fit in. I was the blue-eyed child in a family with brown eyes. The tall kid in a group of shrimps. The woman who cleaned houses for a living while her best friends performed brain surgery or created groundbreaking software or turned Wall Street straw into gold.

I should have stayed behind at the cottage and offered to watch Laria so Chloe could go off searching for Mallory and Ava. She was the one who knew the area. She was the one overflowing with magick. She wouldn't have gotten herself locked in a totaled car like a schmuck.

And that was when the crying started. Like I said, I didn't have a lot of experience when it came to giant bouts of self-pity but it looked like I was about to get some on-the-job training. I did my best to hold back but the dam broke and I was off to the races. I hadn't cried that hard when my husband said he was leaving me for a younger, prettier, more fertile version. And it was one of those ugly cries that leave you looking like you were fighting six hangovers at the same time.

I wondered if Gavan had ever seen a woman in the throes of a crying jag. I wasn't sure if the magicks of his clan cried or if they were too busy doing whatever it was they did all day to make ends meet. I wondered what he would do if he saw me like this. Would he recognize what was happening or would he think I had lost my mind?

He had shown great compassion for Chloe and Luke when he broke off the betrothal and enabled them to marry but what else was going on inside his heart? I knew there was something happening between us, some kind of powerful attraction, but maybe sexual chemistry was as far as it went.

And that made me cry even harder.

Chloe had warned me from the start. "You don't understand the nature of magicks," she had said, her amber eyes dark with concern for my recently-broken heart. "Especially magicks who practice the old ways."

She was talking about Gavan and the elusive happily-ever-after ending we searched for like it was the Holy Grail. Maybe all of that talk about *love conquers all* and *we're all the same inside* was a bunch of crap. Even if Gavan were willing to risk everything to be with me, Rohesia would snuff me out like I was an ant at a picnic. I saw the way she looked at me the few times our paths crossed and it wasn't good. She'd aim her magickal can of Raid in my direction and poof! I'd be history.

Not that it mattered. I was probably going to die of starvation in this minivan before she had the chance to get rid of me.

Or maybe this had been her idea from the start. Nothing like locking a girl up in an abandoned vehicle to show her where she stood in the scheme of things.

Self-pity was pushed aside by good old-fashioned anger. Maybe she could make sure her grandson did her bidding but she had no hold on me. She didn't control my thoughts, my actions, or my future. In fact, she could take her old-world magick and stick it up her magickal butt.

The thought made me laugh out loud. I didn't owe her anything. She wasn't my grandmother or my leader or my friend. She might be ancient and possess powers I could only dream about but I was a red-blooded human female who didn't need magick to make her life complete.

I was just about to nominate myself as the poster child for female empowerment when a young man's face popped up at the side window of the minivan and I let out a horror movie queen scream that they probably heard back in Bailey's Harbor.

I never expected the face to scream back at me and drop from sight.

Now what was I going to do? The guy on the other side of the window was either there to rescue me or kill me. Either way I was helpless, held prisoner in a minivan that wasn't even my own.

A primal rage boiled up from the center of my being and unleashed emotions I didn't know I had. Anger mixed with magick, a potent mix that pushed against the doors and windows, looking for a way out like steam in a pressure cooker.

The face popped up again and this time I didn't scream. It was Janice's son, one of the kids I'd seen causing trouble around town.

"Liam Meany, unlock this car and let me out now!"

"No way," he said. "You're scary."

"You're afraid of a human? I'm surprised at you." I didn't mention my temporary powers. The kid didn't have to know everything.

"I'm not afraid of you." He almost looked like he meant it.

"Good. Then open up this car and let me out."

He shook his head.

"If you're not afraid of me, then what's the problem? You came back to see if I was okay, didn't you?"

"I came back because we pranked the wrong car."

"That's known as a guilty conscience."

"I didn't cause the accident," he said, trying to weasel word his way out of responsibility. "I was just hanging out. It was their idea."

"But you saw it happen and ran away?"

He flushed a deep, angry red and shrugged in that typical teenage way meant to drive anyone over twenty-one crazy. "I didn't exactly see it happen."

"But you knew about it."

104

He nodded. "Yeah. That's why I came back."

"I don't have time for this." I admit it wasn't my finest hour, but I refused to give him any credit at all. He had abandoned a pregnant woman and a little girl. It was hard to find an upside to that. My anger quickly reached volcanic proportions. "Just let me out of here so I can find them before you have three deaths on your hands."

He literally turned white before my eyes. "You think they're--?"

"There's a lot of blood in this car. What do you think happened, Einstein?"

He disappeared from view for a moment. I heard him muttering something in increasingly louder tones, then the doors opened, and I leaped out and jumped him.

"Hey!" he yelled as I slammed him to the snow-covered ground. "What the—"

"Shut up," I snarled, magick flowing from me like a tidal wave. "I don't have time to deal with you now."

That golden cord Gavan had used to bind us together would do nicely.

I trussed the terrified kid like he was a Thanksgiving turkey and flung him into the car headfirst.

"You can't leave me here," he cried, not exactly a big shot now.

"Just watch me, Liam Meany."

"But it's cold."

"You'll live."

"I can help you find your friends."

"You've done enough for me already," I said.

"We didn't mean to hurt anyone," he said again. "We just want you to go away."

"What did I ever do to you?" I had maybe seen the kid three times since the wedding and we had never exchanged a word.

"Everything's different since you showed up," he said. "Those freaks are everywhere." The look he shot me revealed more than he had intended. "And you hang with the big one in that stupid cloak."

"That's none of your business." And there was nothing stupid about Gavan's embroidered cloak. Both were magnificent.

"Nobody wants you here." It was a schoolyard taunt from a spoiled brat kid, but it hurt just the same. Bullies were good at that.

"Then we're even," I said, "because I don't want to be here."

"Why wouldn't you want to be in Sugar Maple?" The idiot kid sounded amazed. After all, everyone had been so welcoming to me.

I slammed the doors shut and watched as my temporary magick wove a shiny silver cage around the car.

"That should hold you for awhile," I said, then aimed another blast of stay-out-of-my-face magick in his direction.

"You're not going to tell my mom, are you?"

I almost laughed out loud. "Oh, you bet I am."

And I was going to enjoy every minute of watching Janice Meany eat crow.

But that pleasure would have to wait. Finding Mallory and Ava was my top priority.

I struck out in the direction of the faint bloodstains, ignoring Liam's pitiful pleas for help. He wasn't getting any more than he deserved. Probably far less than he deserved, if you thought about it. He and his friends had caused two innocent people to crash into a tree during a blizzard. Spending a few uncomfortable hours in the car he had helped wreck didn't seem like unjust punishment for the crime.

The kid definitely had a good set of lungs on him. He howled with outrage over his situation.

"Knock it off," I called over my shoulder. "You sound like a big baby."

That shut him up. The male of the species never disappoints. The kid was tied up and locked in a minivan and he still thought he was the lead sled dog. Maybe he would grow up to be one of those fire-walking, self-help gurus that populate late night TV selling books to teach other people how to become just as obnoxious.

Then again he might escape from the locked minivan and knock me over as he raced by.

I'm ashamed to admit I forgot all about Mallory and Ava. I took off after him at a speed not even magick could explain and I was almost close enough to grab his legs when I was yanked to a full stop six inches off the ground.

"Your timing sucks," I said as Gavan manifested next to me. "I've been yanking that chain for an hour. Where have you been?"

It was a rhetorical question. He'd been searching for Mallory and Ava, while I'd been engaged in a battle of wits with a kid whose voice hadn't fully changed yet. And I was seriously pissed off about that. Reason was gone. I finally understood why men played the "Mine is bigger than yours" game. Liam Meany's magick really was bigger than mine, and the fact that a kid had outsmarted me made me crazy. I launched myself back into pursuit with Gavan right next to me.

"This will not help us find the mother and child," Gavan said as we negotiated a sharp turn around a stand of white birch.

"That little rat and his friends caused the accident," I said, speeding up. "They're not going to get away with it."

"First the mother and child must be found."

I was in no mood for logic. His words slowed me down, but they didn't stop me.

We were heading toward the mountain where Forbes the Giant made his home. Liam had a good lead on us now. Once we got into the densely wooded mountains, our chances of grabbing him would be next to zero. I wondered where he was going. He was heading away from Sugar Maple. Did he have some hiding place outside of town? Were his friends waiting for him?

"Come on," I said, gearing up for an end run. "I'm not going to let him get away. We can surround him before he --"

And then it hit me. Maybe we didn't want to grab him. Maybe what we really wanted to do was follow him straight to where he'd left Mallory and Ava.

Chapter 15

CHLOE

We were deep inside a cave, illuminated only by a soft glow from the imps. Who knew imps doubled as nightlights?

I had been inside caves before and knew I should be grateful for the light they provided. Until you've been inside a cave, you don't know what darkness is all about. The air was damp and cool against my skin, the temperature steady as a heartbeat.

Laria seemed utterly content to be surrounded by those miserable creatures. She wasn't at all surprised to see me come tumbling suddenly into view. She had been expecting me.

I swooped her up into my arms, pushing the hissing, agitated imps aside with my foot. I kissed the top of her head and her chubby cheeks while checking to make sure she was okay. No bumps. No bruises. I whispered my thanks.

The imps were living up to their reputation as Corgi clones, nipping at my ankles and making angry noises meant to scare me away.

"Is this how you treated my mother when I was Laria's age?" I asked. "You should be ashamed."

The nipping and grumbling stopped and they looked up at me.

"I'm her mother," I said, meeting their beady little eyes head-on. "I'm glad you want to keep Laria safe, but never, *never* get in my way." I focused in on each of them in turn. "I'm in charge. You're not. Do you understand?"

The change in them was instantaneous. They literally rolled over and exposed their hairy bellies to me in abject obedience. The sight was both hilarious and more than a little disturbing. I struggled to keep from laughing out loud.

"Are they in this cave?" I asked Laria. "Is that why you brought us here?"

Her little body started to twitch. The imps picked up on her agitation and began running in tight circles around us. We were on the right track.

Two small openings, halfway between floor and ceiling, pierced the otherwise impenetrable wall before us. They stared down on us like dark, unblinking eyes. Stalagmites extended up from the cave floor, joining with thousand-pound stalactites suspended from the ceiling, to form monstrous columns that stood like sentinels guarding each entrance.

Everywhere I looked, random formations of condensation glistened like diamonds in the soft light thrown by the imps. Suddenly, the columns slid back, revealing a third entrance, larger and more foreboding, between them. It dared us to enter.

I thought I caught a faint moan coming from within and I held out a hand to silence everyone so I could zero in on the sound.

A moment later Laria wrenched herself from my arms and flew into the new opening and out of sight with the imps and me in hot pursuit. They looked agitated and apologetic for letting her slip through their circle of protection and I found my hard line attitude softening. She was definitely a handful. We would all have our work cut out for us as she grew stronger and even more powerful.

And, let's face it, I was grateful for the light they provided. I never did like being in the dark. Not even metaphorically.

The beauty of the cave itself almost made up for the fact that I was bouncing off stalagmites and stalactites like a half-human bumper car. Rocks. Minerals. Water. Mix them together, wait a few thousand years or so, and you have magnificence on a scale Tiffany could only dream about.

Just when I thought I couldn't take one more second of navigating my way through the twisting, turning, endless corridor, I skidded to a halt at the entrance to an ice palace so beautiful that I was sure I'd crossed dimensions. The world I knew and loved held vistas of heart-stopping wonder, but this was in a league all its own.

Even the imps stopped chattering and stared, wide-eyed, at the splendor surrounding us.

The immense chamber was a study in contrast: muted shades of amber and pearl and silver interspersed with crystal clear icicles that refracted light like a prism. The colors of the rainbow illuminated the entire area, bouncing off the ceiling and walls. This magnificent show of color and light was thrown back at us by the inky-black reflecting pool that stretched partway across the expanse. Everywhere I looked, every place my gaze landed on, I saw nothing but pure eye candy.

And then it got even better.

There, on the other side of the pool, was Laria with Mallory and Ava.

I sailed across the reflecting pool on a combination of love and magick while the imps, yipping with excitement, happily splashed their way to the other side.

Laria, still clutching Ava's hot pink scrunchie, glowed with joy. She was seated between Ava and Mallory, her tiny body leaning against the child. Ava was asleep with her head resting against Mallory's shoulder.

My relief vanished the moment I saw Mallory up close. Streaks of dried blood bisected her paper white face. Unlike Ava, she wasn't sleeping. She was unconscious, moaning softly with each shaky breath she took.

If only Elspeth were there. Her healing powers were legendary.

She would know what to do. I felt more inadequate than I had ever felt in my life. Life or death decisions can do that to a woman.

When it came to magick, I was still in grade school.

I looked to my baby daughter for help, but she was happily chattering to herself while she played with Ava's scrunchie. She had accomplished her task and all was right in her world.

Unfortunately finding the mother and daughter was only the first step in securing a happy ending.

Mallory was in bad shape. I was no doctor, but I could easily see that we were on shaky ground. Head injuries could be far more deadly than they looked at first glance. I remembered when that beautiful English actress died unexpectedly a few days after a minor fall on a Canadian ski slope. I prayed to the ancestors that the same thing wouldn't happen to Mallory.

And there was her pregnancy to consider. The early months could be fraught with peril. Mallory repeatedly stroked her still-flat belly, but I didn't know if it was a sign of distress or the pregnant woman's universal go-to gesture. Female intuition told me to assume the former and hope for the latter.

I needed help. There was no way I could transport all of us to a hospital. I reached into my pocket for my cell phone. I had a copy of Laria's map but nothing else. I wished I'd had time to think before I launched myself into the Book of Spells in pursuit of Laria.

"Quiet!" I said to the imps. "I can't think with all that hissing and yipping."

They shut up instantly, gathering more closely around my feet, looking up at me with big purple imp eyes.

"Do you know Gavan and Wendy?" I asked the pack.

They did a quick little yes move that reminded me of the Rockettes.

"Find them for me and bring them here as fast as you can."

They looked toward Laria. She stopped playing, met their eyes, and nodded.

Just like that most of them were gone.

Ten months old and she was already comfortable being the one in charge. I had a lot to learn.

Four of the imps had stayed behind to provide light and I was grateful they had thought of it. With their glow spilling over my left shoulder, I crouched down near Mallory, trying to gauge her condition as best I could.

She had sustained a nasty head wound, which scared the hell out of me. Her clothing had been torn. Bits and pieces of leaves and branches clung to what was left of her sweater. Her hands were bloody. A tiny red circle marked her inner wrist. Her shoes had gone missing.

But it was her baby that worried me the most.

Ava woke up and the solace of sleep gave way to fear. She blinked, rubbed her eyes hard, and then saw me.

"You're Laria's mommy," she said, some of the fear disappearing. "She said you would help us."

"I will," I said, giving her a reassuring hug. "We've been looking for you."

"I know," Ava said. "Laria told us."

I asked her how long Mallory had been sleeping. The answer sent a chill up my spine. *Too long.*

"Can you tell me what happened, Ava?"

She was only a little girl, but she did an impressive job of laying out the situation.

"The balloons blew up," she said, eyes wide. "They scared me."

That explained the bruising I saw starting to blossom on Mallory's chest. Air bags saved lives, but they weren't without drawbacks.

"Do you remember where you and your mommy left the car?"

She shook her head. "The big tree came down and we had to go into the forest."

"Did you go deep into the forest?"

She shook her head again. "Not so deep. These people ran out and scared us. That's why Mommy hit the tree."

Despair flooded my heart. "Could you see what they looked like?"

"They were all covered up," she said, "like they were in their bathrobes."

Rohesia's people. There was no other explanation. It killed me that Janice had been right. I owed her an apology.

But first I had to attempt to stabilize Mallory while I waited for help to arrive.

"We're going to wake up your mommy now," I said to Ava.

"You should let her sleep," Ava advised. "She was hurting a whole lot when she was awake."

"This is important, honey," I said. "I promise I won't hurt her."

I searched the deep kangaroo pockets of my sweatshirt for a tissue or something I could use as a wet cloth to moisten Mallory's lips. The only thing I found was the folded-up copy of Laria's map. It slipped from my fingers and dropped into the pool lapping at my feet.

"Rats," I muttered, getting down on my hands and knees to pluck it from the cool, clear water. I leaned forward, stretching to reach the map.

"What's that?" Ava asked.

"A map," I said, wiggling my fingers closer to the soggy page.

"What's a map?"

"A drawing that shows you where you are in the world."

"Like a globe?" she asked.

"But flat," I said. "Your mommy probably uses one when she drives."

Ava shook her head. "My mommy uses her cell phone. A voice tells us where to go."

Which was probably how they had ended up in this predicament. Without her cell phone, Mallory had no way to figure out where they were.

I had just managed to pinch a corner of the map between my thumb and index finger when something caught my eye and I stopped cold.

Reflected in the center of the pool of crystal-clear water was another map. The vague outlines resembled the one Laria had drawn but this was more detailed, more perfectly rendered.

"What?" Ava crawled over toward me on the slippery rocks. "What do you see?"

"I'm not sure," I said, glancing over at her. "What do you see?"

"Water," she said, "and some rocks."

"You don't see a drawing of a pretty town with lots of trees?"

She shook her head. "Nope, just water."

The vision was part map, part folk art, much like the centuries-old piece of birch bark Lilith kept in the library. The bark dated back to the time when our Salem ancestors joined with the Abenaki Indians and Sugar Maple was born. The earliest layout of our town was there, small houses and wigwams, but so were stars and moons and waterfalls, all the iconic images that came to represent the place I called home.

I looked up at the natural ceiling of the chamber but there were no clues there, only the smooth and glowing beauty of the rock formations.

I pulled out Laria's map and spread it out on one of the rocks next to me and gasped in surprise.

The earnest scribbles of a child had been replaced with a perfect representation of the image reflected back to me from the surface of the pool of water.

This wasn't a coincidence. I was being shown this rendering of early Sugar Maple for a reason. But figuring out what the reason was would have to wait.

I soaked the sleeve of my sweatshirt in the cool water of the reflecting pool then dabbed Mallory's mouth with it. She stirred slightly. I filled my cupped hands with more water and brought the water to her lips. Ava understood what I was doing and she urged her mom to open her mouth and sip. I wasn't sure how much Mallory understood, but we did manage to get some liquid into her which had to be a good thing.

"How did you and your mom find this cave?" I asked Ava as I continued to urge more water on Mallory.

"The lady took us here."

"What lady?" I asked.

"I don't know her name," Ava said, "but she was really pretty."

"What did she look like?"

Ava thought for a moment. "Like an old Disney princess," she said, "except she was wearing a fancy blanket in all sorts of colors."

Rohesia? Nobody else in Sugar Maple fit that description. To say I was gobsmacked is putting it mildly. How did Rohesia even know of Mallory's and Ava's existence? Maybe this was nothing more than childhood imagination gone crazy.

Mallory wouldn't take more water, no matter how much Ava begged. She drifted back into a semi-conscious state, which upset the little girl even more.

It was hard to remember a time when I felt more helpless. There was nothing we could do but wait and hope Gavan and Wendy showed up soon. I had depleted some of my own magick when I granted Wendy temporary powers and wasn't sure I could transport both Mallory and Ava safely to the hospital. And I wasn't about to leave Ava alone in the cave or give Laria free rein to sail through a blizzard.

All along I had believed that once we found Mallory and Ava, we'd have our happy ending but now, for the first time, I was starting to think that maybe I was wrong.

Chapter 16

WENDY

We were staying close behind Liam Meany when Gavan abandoned the chase, veered left and then plunged deeper into the woods.

"Stop!" I hollered after Gavan. "We're supposed to be following him!"

Had he somehow zeroed in on Mallory and Ava? That was the only possible reason I could come up with for the sudden change of direction.

I veered left too and caught up with Gavan, skidding to a stop a few feet shy of a few dozen purple-eyed creatures the likes of which I'd never seen before.

"Imps," Gavan said, hovering next to me. "Laria sent them."

"They're imps? They look like two-legged dogs." They sounded like them as well, all shrill yips and breathy chortles. And was I crazy or did they smell like cinnamon? I had imagined imps to be cute little characters with big smiles and mischievous personalities. These were chubby Chihuahuas in need of manscaping.

They led us across a tiny stream and stopped at the opening to a cave.

"Do you trust them?" I asked, remembering Chloe's negative reaction at the mere mention of the creatures.

"Yes," he said. "They are Laria's guardians."

In for a penny, in for a pound.

We followed the imps through the cave entrance and deep into the cavern beyond, guided by the light shining from their hairy little bodies.

My grandparents used to take us on car trips every summer. We visited all manner of natural wonders, from Niagara Falls to the Grand Canyon and everything in between. But they loved caverns most of all. We must have visited Howe Cavern at least five times while I was growing up.

I thought I knew what to expect. So it came as a jaw-dropping surprise when we stepped into a massive cathedral of shimmering stalagmites and stalactites that seemed to soar to the heavens. The caves I'd visited had been commercialized with fairy lights and laser shows and enough showmanship to impress P. T. Barnum. This was nature at her most raw and beautiful and it took my breath away.

Gavan, however, was unimpressed by the cavern. His attention was focused on more important things. "Look," he said, pointing across a pool of clear water.

My heart soared! Mallory and Ava were safe and sound. Gavan's decision to abandon the chase for Liam Meany had definitely been the right one.

We sailed across the pool the same way we had sailed over the snow. The imps splashed and grumbled their way through the water like disgruntled children. My elation quickly downshifted to fear when I saw the condition Mallory was in.

My eyes met Chloe's. She made an "I don't know" face, taking care that Ava wasn't watching. A tight knot formed in my stomach. It was terrifyingly clear that Mallory was in bad shape, but how were we going to transport an injured pregnant human through miles of heavy snow to reach a hospital. I hoped somebody had the answer, because Mallory needed help now.

I turned away so Ava couldn't see the worry on my face, letting my gaze travel around the cathedral-like space. The walls shimmered as if an unseen hand had applied Swarovski crystals to every available space. People talked about crystal-clear water, but it wasn't often that you actually saw it. Intrigued, I leaned forward and gasped when I saw something that reminded me of Laria's map reflected with mirror-like clarity. I wasn't sure why this detailed rendering of what appeared to be an Indian village from hundreds of years ago reminded me of a baby's scribbles, so I pulled my copy of the map from my pocket, unfolded it, and almost tumbled headfirst into the pool of water.

It was an exact match, down to every last blade of grass.

I'm not sure what happened or when but somehow Laria's attempt at map-making had morphed into a folk art display. Chalk up another win for magick.

But there wasn't time to consider the implications. The rescue operation was in full swing and Gavan was leading the way.

Three humans, one of whom was pregnant and injured. A baby with powers. Two adults with varying degrees and styles of magick. A foot of snow outside. No working phones or transportation.

I could see the fear in Chloe's eyes each time she looked at Mallory. Head injuries could be unpredictable and I knew the dangers that grew with every minute that passed.

"I will take Mallory to the hospital," Gavan said. "Laria asked two of the imps to show me the way."

Once again, Baby to the rescue. I couldn't believe I was jealous of someone who was still in diapers, but there you had it.

"I'll go with you," I said. "You'll need help navigating the admissions process."

He shook his head. "I can transport only the woman. My magick is not powerful enough to safely transport another."

"You forget that I have magick too."

"Not any more," Chloe piped up. "The spell I cast will wear off in about ten minutes."

"Then weave me another one."

"I wish I could," Chloe said. "Temporary spells come with restrictions. One per human, per day."

"So how is this going to play out?"

"I'm going with Gavan and Mallory," Chloe said. "You're right about him needing help navigating the hospital's red tape."

"That's good for you and for Gavan and Mallory," I said, "but where does that leave me?"

"You're going to drive Laria and Ava to join us at the hospital."

"In what?" I asked. "A giant snow plow?"

One thing about my cousin: she can seem a bit scatterbrained but don't let that fool you. The woman can work a problem with the best of them. While Gavan and I were making our way to the cave, she had rallied a band of house sprites and set them on a search for Mallory's wrecked minivan. According to Chloe, they had not only brought it back to showroom condition, they had driven it to the mouth of the cave where it was waiting for me to drive the kids to the hospital.

"Did you have them plow the roads too?" I asked.

"I might have called in a favor or two."

I lowered my voice so Ava couldn't hear me. "How bad off is Mallory?"

Chloe frowned. "I'm not sure she'll make it to the hospital."

To my horror, my eyes welled with tears I struggled to control.

"I'll worry about getting Mallory to the hospital. You take care of the girls." Chloe gave me a swift hug. "They're everything."

Chapter 17

CHLOE

We had been waiting for hours at the hospital for news on Mallory when the E.R. doctor approached our group.

She wasn't smiling.

"Mrs. Hobbs?" I didn't correct her. "I'm afraid we have a problem."

The room went still. I'm not sure any of us drew a breath. Ava had been given a thorough exam and pronounced cold, tired, but very healthy. She and Laria were sleeping soundly on one of the big vinyl couches, tucked in with blankets and pillows and even a portable car seat for the baby, courtesy of the nurses' station. Gavan and Wendy sat on either side of the two little girls, watching over them.

"How serious?" I asked.

"We aren't sure. We haven't been able to fully examine Mrs. Grant," the doctor said.

"It's been over an hour," I said, a tad more sharply than I had intended. "We're the only ones in emergency. What's the hold-up?"

She actually looked embarrassed. "We seem to be having a hospital-wide power glitch."

"The lights are still on," I observed. "Are you talking internet problems?"

"I wish that were the only problem," she said. "Radiology is down, as well as the labs, and because the internet is down, we can't access the patient's records to provide guidance."

"I guess the storm hit us all hard," I said.

"That's the weird part. The storm has been going on for hours, but our troubles just began a few minutes ago. We considered Medevac for Mrs. Grant, but our problem currently makes it impossible for the helicopter to land safely."

Old magick strikes again, I thought.

"You must have made a preliminary diagnosis," I prodded. "I mean, you have to know something."

She bristled. I didn't blame her, but her reaction still annoyed me. After all, I wasn't the one with M.D. after my name.

"Her injuries may or may not be life-threatening. We don't think they are, but at this point it's only an educated guess. What I do know is that the pregnancy is in jeopardy," she said, "but that's all I can tell you at this juncture."

"Then do something," I demanded. "Doctors saved lives before CT scans and MRIs, didn't they? There must be something you can do."

"We're doing all we can," the doctor said, as her throat and cheeks burned bright red. "We'll keep you informed of any changes."

The woman fled the room like her shoes were on fire. I didn't blame her. My anger was volcanic. I could have laid waste to the waiting room with one wave of my hand.

Shaking with rage, I turned on Gavan. "You have to get out of here," I ordered. "We're losing her and it's all your fault."

No explanations were necessary. He and Wendy had heard the exchange, loud and clear. Once again the old magick was clashing with the modern world with disastrous results.

Gavan looked stricken and I softened. He was a good man. I

had learned that on my wedding day when he stepped aside and gave me back my future with Luke.

"I know you didn't mean for any of this to happen, but it has. Your magick is screwing everything up. As long as you're in this hospital, they can't run tests on Mallory and that puts Mallory and her baby in terrible jeopardy."

He nodded and stood up.

"All will be as it should be," he said and walked out the door.

"I'm going with him," Wendy said and I nodded. If the tables had been turned and it was Luke walking out the door, I would have done the same thing.

~

WENDY

Gavan was waiting for me in the hallway.

"Come on," I said, reaching for his hand. "We need to get far enough away so their electronics can get back on line."

"No," he said. "You must take me to Mallory."

"You don't understand," I said. "Your magick is causing trouble. You need to get out of here so they can take care of her."

"My absence will not help her but my magick will."

"I'm not following you."

"It was Rohesia who brought them to the cave and kept them safe." He had noticed a small red circle on the inside of Ava's and Mallory's right wrists, the ancient mark of protection within his clan.

"Rohesia cast a spell on them?"

"A charm," he corrected me. "To protect her against danger from other magicks."

"The Sugar Maples."

He nodded. "That is so."

I quickly did the math. The old magick charm had also thrown a monkey wrench into the hospital's electronic systems. "So why don't you undo it?"

"Only Rohesia can undo it." He would ask her to reverse it once Mallory was out of the woods.

"But you think you can get around the charm and heal Mallory."

"There is no other choice. Her baby's time grows short."

"Why didn't Rohesia heal them?"

"She hasn't the knowledge. Humans remain a mystery to her."

"And we're not a mystery to you?"

"Elspeth has been sharing her knowledge with me. If we are to make a success here in your world, we must learn." He gave his version of a shrug. "Elspeth is a fine teacher."

"Okay, then," I said. "Let's try radiology."

The hospital was quiet. The blizzard had reduced staffing to a skeleton crew. I would have expected the emergency room to be overrun with people but the storm had slowed the world down to a crawl. I led the way down a darkened corridor, nodding hello as we passed a young doctor in blue scrubs.

"Can I help you with anything?" she asked, her eyes focused on Gavan.

"The cafeteria," I said. "We need coffee bad."

She laughed, still staring up at Gavan. "Well, bad coffee is what you'll get."

She gave us directions to the cafeteria then hurried on her way.

"You really need to work on blending in," I said to him as we followed the signs to radiology. "You're just too—" I started to say *beautiful* but managed to stop myself. "It might be time to retire that cloak."

He removed it and draped it across my shoulders. It smelled of him, of fresh air and pine and the sea, and for a second I felt dizzy with pleasure.

"Is this better?" he asked. He was wearing close-fitting trousers and a black t-shirt. Just your average, everyday Adonis.

"It's worse," I said, aware that every woman in the hospital and

BARBARA BRETTON

a fair number of the men would have him in their sights, "but we'll go with it."

The hospital was eerily empty. I had to assume that most of the staff was busy on the patient floors, which was a lucky break for us. The young doctor in scrubs was the last person we bumped into before we found the door to radiology.

I pushed it open. The administrative area was dark and silent. Gavan stood in the middle of the room, his head tilted slightly to the left, and listened.

"Come on," I said. "She's not here."

He didn't respond, just stood there with his head tilted like a dog on the hunt.

"Time's running out," I said. "Let's go."

He grabbed my hand in his and the next thing I knew, we were standing at the foot of Mallory's bed on the surgical floor. A lone nurse was holding fort at the far end of the hallway, doing whatever it was she had to do on the computer.

"She cannot see or hear us," Gavan said in answer to my unspoken question. "We are shielded from observation."

Mallory was surrounded by a variety of machines, none of which were working. Her clothes were neatly folded on a chair near the window. The stark whiteness of the hospital gown she wore matched the whiteness of her skin. She looked far worse than she had a few hours ago when we found her in the cave.

"Mallory." Gavan's voice was low. "We are here to help you."

She moaned softly. Her eyes fluttered open and her gaze moved from Gavan to me then back again "Who--?"

I stepped forward. "I'm Wendy. This is Gavan. He brought you here from the cave."

She struggled to sit up but lacked the strength and fell back against the small pillow. "Ava," she managed. "Where is she?"

"She's in the waiting room with Chloe," I said. "She's asleep."

A quick smile illuminated her face.

"The baby?" she whispered. "I heard them talking ..."

Gavan took her hands in his and I could feel the power of magick light the room.

"Your son will make you proud," he said, his words visible in the air between us. "He will be strong like his father. He will be kind like his mother. He will question the world like his sister. He will live to know the children of his children's children."

I couldn't have stopped the tears flowing down my cheeks if I tried. Maybe I was crazy but I believed every word he said. I believed he could pull Mallory back from a fate she didn't deserve and give her back her future.

I believed that, for the first time in my life, I was really in love.

∾

MALLORY

"Mrs. Grant." The voice floated toward Mallory from somewhere near the ceiling. "Mallory. Wake up. We need to run a few tests."

Mallory had been drifting between sleep and wakefulness. Each time she awoke, she felt more like herself. The pain had dwindled to almost nothing and a deep sense of gratitude had taken its place.

"I'm fine," she managed, pushing herself up on her elbows. "I just want to see my daughter."

"You may very well be fine," the technician attached to the voice said, "but until we run some tests, we can't confirm it."

"He said I was fine," Mallory persisted.

"Who told you that you were fine?"

"The man who came in here." She searched for a name but came up blank. "He was a doctor, I think. There was a woman with him."

The technician laughed. "You were dreaming," she said. "Nothing wrong with that."

Mallory knew she hadn't been dreaming, but she let it go. "I still want to see my daughter."

"After we run the tests, you can see your daughter."

"If I don't see my daughter, I'm going to check myself out of here."

That did it.

Two minutes later, a sleepy Ava was curled up on the narrow bed next to Mallory.

"Look at those pajamas!" Mallory exclaimed. "Where did they come from?"

"The nurse gave them to me," Ava said around a yawn. "Pink is my favorite color."

Everybody knew Ava's favorite color was pink. "I've never seen pink elephants before."

"The nurse said they were special." Ava yawned again. "My sticker is gone," she said, looking at the inside of her wrist. "It was pretty."

"You had a sticker?"

"You had one too," Ava said, her eyes drooping, "but now it's gone." Another gigantic yawn. "I'm sleepy."

"Close your eyes," Mallory said, pulling the light cover up over her daughter's shoulders. "I'm here with you."

And I always will be.

Chapter 18

CHLOE

"My in-laws are a half hour away," Mallory said as she put down her cell phone. "Ava will be so excited."

"The doctors are going to release you?" I asked, sipping my cup of dusty hospital tea.

Mallory grinned at me over her glass of orange juice. "They wanted me to stay one more night but that's not going to happen."

"It might not be a bad idea."

"I'm fine, Chloe. Trust me. That doctor was positive."

"You mean Dr. Schulman?"

"I don't know his name."

"Dr. Schulman is a woman."

"I know. I'm talking about the doctor who came to see me in my room earlier."

"A tall, great-looking guy?"

"I didn't notice. I was still pretty woozy." She thought for a moment. "The woman with him seemed familiar."

I nodded. The puzzle pieces were beginning to fall into place.

"What exactly did he do?"

"That's the funny thing. I'm not sure he did anything but I started to feel better the moment he took my hands."

I took a quick look at the inside of her right wrist. The red circle that had been present on her wrist, as well as Ava's and Laria's, was gone. I knew from the Book of Spells that the protective charms used by old magicks back in the day were tattooed to the inner wrist of the recipient.

I was sure we had both Rohesia and Gavan to thank for the happy ending. What could have been a tragedy had turned out to be a celebration.

Laria and Ava were happily playing in the corner of the room. The nurses had been unbelievably kind to us, providing the girls with toys and food and a DVD player that played *Frozen* over and over until Mallory and I thought we were going to go crazy. But it was a good crazy. Luke would be here any moment. Ava and Mallory would be with their family again. And I guessed Gavan and Wendy would catch up with me once I was away from the hospital.

I was about to take a bite of cold pancake when Mallory looked up from her french toast.

"Do you believe in magic?"

Uh-oh.

"Magic?" I asked.

"Well, maybe not magic exactly," she qualified. "If I tell you something, do you promise you won't think I'm crazy?"

"Depends on what you tell me," I said with what I hoped was a casual chuckle.

"I don't think he was really a doctor." She lowered her voice. "In fact, I think the woman he was with works at your shop."

Okay. Now we were definitely venturing into dangerous territory.

"That's my cousin Wendy," I explained in a matter-of-fact voice. "She drove Ava to the hospital."

Mallory's eyes widened and I realized my mistake. "Who drove me to the hospital?"

"I did." It was only a partial lie. Gavan and I got her here but it definitely wasn't by car.

"I don't remember that."

"I wouldn't worry about it, Mallory. You were in and out of consciousness. Things are bound to get confused."

"But it seemed so real," she said. "He took my hands and told me I was having a boy."

"Are you?"

She shrugged. "Still too soon to know."

"I think you were dreaming," I said. "Your imagination pulled in all sorts of images and conversations and created a storyline."

"I guess," she said, not sounding at all convinced.

We polished off the rest of the hospital breakfast and I had just started to stack the plates and dishes on a tray when we heard the sound of footsteps rushing along the corridor and a tall, handsome couple burst into the room.

Ava shrieked with delight and threw herself at her grandparents. "Grammy! Gramps!" she shouted, tackling them around the knees. "Mommy said you were coming!"

Mallory was so happy that she started to cry, which (of course) got me started crying too. Laria woke up from her post-nursing nap and decided to join in the fun.

I doubt if anyone but Ava noticed when I scooped up Laria and eased toward the door. The two little girls exchanged last looks and I wondered if I would ever really understand the bond that had formed between them.

Laria fussed all the way down to the main floor. The elevator shimmied into position and I stepped into the sun-filled lobby. Why is it that the day after a major storm is always heartbreakingly beautiful? One of the many mysteries of life.

The other mystery was how Laria and I were going to get home.

"Need a lift?" asked a familiar voice.

I turned slowly and met Janice's eyes. Her timing had always been terrific. "Are you offering one?"

"That and an apology or two," she said. "Liam has something to say to you."

I hadn't noticed her son standing off to her left.

Wendy and Gavan had been right. The younger Sugar Maples had been engaged in a hormonally-charged teenage turf war.

"They came in and took over everything," Liam said, sounding righteously outraged. "The cave's our place. It goes back to when it was part of Sinzibukwud. They can find somewhere else to hook up."

I exchanged glances with Janice. "Did you ever use the cave to--?"

Janice shook her head. "Did you?"

"Have we met? I didn't date until I was almost twenty-one." Tall, skinny, and socially inept was not a recipe for dating success.

"We were trying to scare your cousin," Liam continued. "We didn't want to hurt her. We figured she would tell the big guy and maybe we could drive them out."

"You could have killed two innocent people, Liam," I said. "Do you realize that?"

"I'm sorry," he said. "Really sorry. That's why I'm here. I wanted to see if they were okay."

"No thanks to you and your friends," I said, still not quite ready to let him off the hook. "It was Rohesia who gave them shelter and kept them safe until we found them."

"Seriously?" Janice asked, eyebrows raised.

I nodded. "Seriously."

"I guess I got that one wrong," she said.

"I guess we all did."

Laria woke up from her after-breakfast nap and beamed a great smile at all of us. She reached out her arms to Liam and I only hesitated a moment before I handed her to him. His mother's eyes filled with tears. (So did Liam's but we pretended we didn't notice.) My daughter definitely loved the boys.

"You were right about one thing," I said to Janice as we walked along the shoveled path to the parking lot. "I *have* changed."

Janice nodded, glancing over at me. "You're a mom now," she said. "That changes a woman."

I patted my belly and rolled my eyes. "Tell me about it."

"There's that," she said as we approached her car, "but that's not what I meant." She pulled in a shaky breath. "I know how selfish this sounds, but for thirty years we were everything to you. We were your family." She stopped for a moment and regrouped. "Now you have your own powers. You have a daughter and a family of your own and –" She shrugged. "We miss you."

"I miss you, too." First-time motherhood was a deep dive into family life. Juggling the baby, a husband, the knit shop, and my position as Sugar Maple's *de facto* mayor left little time for the friendships that had sustained me all my life. "I'm going to do better."

"You're doing fine," Janice said as I slid into the passenger seat. "Maybe Lynette and I need to make a few adjustments, too."

"I'm going to look into what's been happening between us and Rohesia's clan." I glanced over my shoulder at Liam who was strapping Laria into one of Janice's old car seats. "I could use your help, Liam, when I do."

His face turned bright red and he nodded. I was pretty sure he wouldn't make the same mistakes again. At least, I hoped not.

"Thank you," Janice said quietly as she headed out of the parking lot.

"I hear he comes from a good family."

The sun was high in the sky when Janice stopped at the foot of my driveway where I'd left the Buick.

"I assume there's a car under there somewhere," she said, flashing me her trademark wicked grin. "Need some help shoveling out? I have a son who could use the practice."

I had to hand it to Liam. He didn't so much as utter a whimper of protest.

"Mother Nature put it there," I said. "I'll let Mother Nature get it out."

Full sun. Temps in the high fifties. It would take no time at all. Besides, who was I kidding? I probably wouldn't drive again until spring.

Liam released Laria from the car seat. She fussed a little when he handed her over to me but settled happily against my shoulder.

"When do you expect Luke?" Janice asked as we said goodbye.

"Any time," I said, aware of the big smile spreading across my face.

"Enjoy," she said, gunning the engine. "Honeymoons don't last very long."

Maybe not, I thought as Laria and I waved goodbye, but I was glad true friendships did.

~

Luke and I were lying in bed with the curtains opened wide to the night. Moonlight spilled across the snow, throwing shadows along the walls of our bedroom.

Across the hall, our daughter slept soundly under the watchful eye of Elspeth, her troll-warrior nanny.

The cats were curled up on the window seat, nestled deep in the folds of the granny afghan I had crocheted when I was eight years old.

We were warm and safe and together and for a moment I believed we would stay that way forever. That's one of the things love did to you. Love softened the rough edges of life. It cushioned the blows. It made you believe dreams really could come true.

And maybe they did. Mallory had texted me a few hours ago to let me know that her husband Josh had been granted humanitarian leave and would be joining her and Ava within the next few days. I was over the moon with pleasure that I had played even a very small part in the outcome.

"You know what this is all about, don't you?" Luke asked as we savored the afterglow.

I whispered something in his ear and he laughed.

"True," he said, "but that's not what I was talking about." He leaned up on one elbow. "You saw yourself in Mallory and Ava."

"We're nothing alike," I protested. "She's human. I'm magick. She—"

"You didn't want Ava to lose her mother the way you lost yours."

And just like that it started to fall into place for me. I knew how it felt to be a little girl without a mother. I didn't want that to happen to Ava.

"That explains my feelings," I said, "but how does Laria figure into this?"

"I'm guessing she made the connection on her own," he said. "You and Laria shared a goal but for different reasons."

"Her powers scare me," I whispered. "I don't know where they're going to take her."

"Imagine how I feel," he said. "I go away for a few days and our baby girl turns into a cartographer/sleuth."

I tried to laugh with him but I was too filled with emotion. "Sometimes I think she's just passing through, that I'm going to wake up one morning and she'll be on her way to some destiny I know nothing about."

Luke, who had lost his first child to an accident before we met, didn't argue the point. "Nobody knows how much time they've got. We're all just passing through, Chloe. That's what makes the good times so sweet."

All around us things were changing at the speed of light. The world seemed to be reinventing itself on an hourly basis and Sugar Maple was no exception. But the things that remained were the things that mattered, the ties of family and friendship.

Magick or human, our time in this dimension was limited. The ride might be a long one, like Elspeth's. It might be poignantly short like my mother's. It might be a life of human dimensions or magick parameters. It was anybody's guess.

I couldn't see into the future. According to the Book of Spells, Laria's destiny has yet to be written. I prayed Luke and I would be together to celebrate a golden anniversary, but the Fates might have other plans for us.

And Sugar Maple? Change was in the wind here, too, and we had to find a way to face those changes together or say goodbye to three hundred years of peace and prosperity.

Luke was right when he said this life came with no guarantees. I guess sometimes it took a human heart to understand all that was invisible to magick. You couldn't see love. You couldn't hear it or smell it or touch it or taste it. But it was there just the same, supporting you during the good times and making the tough times that much more bearable.

When all was said and done, the only thing you could do was hold on tight to the ones you loved and enjoy the ride.

And that was exactly what I planned to do.

The End

Enraptured – The Holiday Story

THE SUGAR MAPLE CHRONICLES - BOOK 7

Coming in October 2018

When a radar glitch brings down billionaire amateur archaeologist Jack Winchester's small plane in the middle of Sugar Maple's First Annual Holiday Street Fair, Jack finds himself hot on the trail of the town's magickal secrets . . . and a rival for the love of a very special woman.

The Secret Language of Knitting

The knitting vocabulary can be confusing to civilians (a.k.a. muggles) so here's a short glossary to help get you up to speed.

BIND OFF - See "cast off"

BSJ - Baby Surprise Jacket, probably EZ's most popular design

CAST OFF - To secure your last row of stitches so they don't unravel

CAST ON - To place a foundation row of stitches on your needle

DPN - Double-pointed needles

EZ - Elizabeth Zimmermann, the knitting mother of us all

FAIR ISLE - Multistranded colorwork

FO - Finished object

FROG - To undo your knitting by ripping back ("Rip it! Rip it!") row by row with great abandon

KITCHENER - Grafting two parallel rows of live stitches to form an invisible seam

KNIT - The basic stitch from which everything derives

KNITALONG - An online phenomenon wherein hundreds of knitters embark on a project simultaneously and exchange progress reports along the way

KUREYON - A wildly popular self-striping yarn created and manufactured by Eisaku Noro under the Noro label

LYS - Local yarn shop

MAGIC LOOP - Knitting a tube with one circular needle instead of four or five double-pointed needles

PURL - The knit stitch's sister—instead of knitting into the back of the stitch with the point of the needle facing away from you, you knit into the front of the stitch with the point of the needle facing directly at you

RAVELRY - An online community for knitters and knitwear designers that has surpassed all expectations

ROVING - What you have after a fleece has been washed, combed, and carded; roving is then ready to be spun into yarn

SABLE - Stash Amassed Beyond Life Expectancy—in other words, you won't live long enough to knit it all!

SEX - Stash Enhancement eXercise—basically spending too much money on way too much yarn

STASH - The yarn you've been hiding in the empty oven, clean trash bins, your basement, your attic, under the beds, in closets, wherever you can keep your treasures clean, dry, and away from critical eyes

STITCH 'N' BITCH - A gathering of like-minded knitters who share knitting techniques and friendship with a twenty-first-century twist

STRANDED - See "Fair Isle"

TINK - To carefully undo your knitting stitch by stitch. Basically to unknit your way back to a mistake-free area

YARN CRAWL - The knitter's equivalent of a pub crawl. Substitute yarn shops for bars and you'll get the picture

Who's Who in Sugar Maple

THE RESIDENTS

CHLOE HOBBS - The half-human, half-sorceress de facto mayor of Sugar Maple and owner of Sticks & Strings, a wildly successful knit shop. As the descendant of sorceress Aerynn, the town's founder, Chloe holds the fate of the magickal town in her hands.

LUKE MACKENZIE - The 100 percent human chief of police. He came to Sugar Maple to investigate the death of Suzanne Marsden, an old high school friend, but stayed because he fell in love with Chloe.

PYEWACKET, BLOT, DINAH, LUCY - Chloe's house cats.

PENELOPE - Chloe's store cat. Penny is actually much more than that. She has been a familiar of the Hobbs women for over three centuries and has often served as a conduit between dimensions.

ELSPETH - A three-hundred-something-year-old troll from Salem who kept house for Samuel Bramford. She has been sent to Sugar Maple to watch over Chloe until the baby is born.

JANICE MEANY - Chloe's closest friend and owner of Cut &

Curl, the salon across the street from Sticks & Strings. Janice is a Harvard-educated witch, descended from a long line of witches. She and her husband, Lorcan, have five children.

LORCAN MEANY - Janice's husband. Lorcan is a selkie and one of Luke's friends.

LYNETTE PENDRAGON - A shifter and owner, with her husband, Cyrus, of Sugar Maple Arts Players. They have five children: Vonnie, Iphigenia, Troy (originally named Gilbert), Adonis (originally named Sullivan), and Will.

LILITH - A Norwegian troll who is Sugar Maple's town librarian and historian. She is married to Archie. Her mother was Sorcha the Healer, who cared for Chloe after her parents died.

MIDGE STALLWORTH - A rosy-cheeked vampire who runs the funeral home with her husband, George.

RENATE WEAVER - Member of the Fae and owner of the Sugar Maple Inn. Renate and her husband, Colm, have four grown children: Bettina, Daisy, Penelope, and Calliope.

BETTINA WEAVER LEONIDES - Harpist, member of the Fae, occasional part-time worker at Sticks & Strings. Married to Alexander. Mother of three children: Memphis, Athens, Ithaca.

PAUL GRIGGS - Werewolf and owner of Griggs Hardware. He is Luke's closest friend in town. He is married to Verna and has two sons: Jeremy and Adam. His nephew Johnny is a frequent visitor.

FRANK - One of the more garrulous vampire retirees at Sugar Maple Assisted Living.

MANNY - Another vampire retiree who pals around with Frank.

ROSE - Frank's and Manny's love interest. She is also a retired vampire who resides at Sugar Maple Assisted Living.

SAMUEL - A four-hundred-plus-year-old wizard who pierced the veil at the end of *Spun by Sorcery*. He was Aerynn's lover and the father of the Hobbs clan.

SORCHA - The healer who stayed behind in the mortal world to raise Chloe to adulthood after her parents died in a car crash. Sorcha is Lilith's birth mother.

AERYNN - A powerful sorceress from Salem who led the magickal creatures from Salem to freedom during the infamous Witch Trials. A gifted spinner, she founded Sinzibukwud in northern Vermont (later renamed Sugar Maple) and passed her magick and her spinning and knitting skills down to generations of Hobbs women. Aerynn is responsible for the magick charm that enables Sugar Maple to hide in plain sight.

GUINEVERE - Chloe's sorceress mother. Guinevere chose to pierce the veil after the auto accident that took her beloved husband's life.

TED AUBRY - Chloe's human father and Guinevere's husband. He was a carpenter by trade. Ted was in medical school when he met Guinevere but gave it up to be with her. A very romantic story until Chloe learned her mother had cast a spell on him to bind him to her.

ISADORA - The most powerful member of the Fae. She is also the most dangerous. Currently Isadora is banished from this realm until the end of time but who knows what the future might bring.

GUNNAR - The good twin, he sacrificed himself so Chloe and Luke could be together.

DANE - The ultimate evil twin.

THE HARRIS FAMILY - They were carpenters in life (c. 1860) but now inhabit the spirit world.

THE SOUDERBUSH BOYS - Father Benjamin, mother Amelia, and sons David, William, and John are all ghosts who spend a lot of time on the Spirit Trail, which passes through the Sugar Maple Inn.

SIMONE - A seductive spirit who specializes in breaking up happy marriages. She usually manifests herself in a wisteria-scented lilac cloud.

FORBES THE MOUNTAIN GIANT - His name pretty much says it all.

THE NEW NEIGHBORS

ROHESIA OF OLWYN – Leader of a clan of Others who

have lived for centuries in a dimension beyond the mist that has reached the end of its natural life.

GAVAN OF ERES – Rohesia's grandson. He is a warrior who was betrothed to Chloe when they were children. He was sent to Sugar Maple to stop her marriage to Luke.

CHLOE'S COUSIN

WENDY AUBRY LATTIMER – A second cousin (a few times removed) via Chloe's human father Ted Aubry. She is young, divorced, and a great knitter.

THE MACKENZIE CLAN

BUNNY - Matriarch, knitter, retired nurse. Born and raised in the Boston suburbs near Salem.

JACK - Patriarch, sport fisherman, retired welder. Also born and raised in the Boston suburbs near Salem.

RONNIE - A successful Realtor, father of four. Married to Denise. He still lives in the town where he was born and raised.

KIMBERLY - Luke's oldest sister. Kim is a financial analyst, married, mother of one with husband Travis Davenport. They have been married nine years. She and Chloe formed an easy bond right from the start.

JENNIFER - Another of Luke's older sisters. She's married to Paul and mother of Diandra, Sean, and Colin.

KEVIN - Luke's younger brother. He has been married to Tiffany for nine years. They have four children: Ami, Honor, Scott, and Michael.

PATRICK - Another younger brother. He's newly divorced from Siobhan. They have two daughters: Caitlin and Sarah.

MEGHAN - The wild card of the bunch. Meghan is the youngest of Bunny and Jack's children and the least predictable. (Her two-minutes younger twin died at birth.) She has the habit of taking up with the wrong guys and paying for it with a broken heart.

FRAN KELLY - Retired administrative assistant to Boston's police chief. Close friend of the MacKenzie family.

STEFFIE - Luke's daughter, who was six years old when she died in a bicycle accident.

KAREN - Luke's ex-wife, who sacrificed herself to save their daughter's soul.

JOE RANDAZZO - County Board of Supervisors; a politician who is an occasional thorn in Chloe's side.

Also by Barbara Bretton

Collections - Anthologies

Now and Forever: The Complete Crosse Harbor Trilogy

Happily Ever After: Three Complete Romances

Happily Ever After 2: Five Complete Romances

Home Front: Three novels of love, war, and family

The Rocky Hill Holiday Collection: Two novels and two novellas

Untamed Hearts: Three complete historical romances

Second Time Around: Two wedding novellas

The PAX Collection – 4 novels of romance and adventure

The Sugar Maple Chronicles – 4 Book Collection

The Jersey Strong Romance Collection – 6 Novels

The Wilde Sisters

Operation: Husband

Operation: Baby

Operation: Family (not yet released)

Bachelor Fathers

Daddy's Girl

The Bride Came C.O.D.

The Crosse Harbor Time Travel Trilogy

Somewhere in Time

Tomorrow & Always

Destiny's Child

Now and Forever: The Complete Crosse Harbor Trilogy

Pax Romantic Adventure Series

Playing for Time

Honeymoon Hotel

A Fine Madness

All We Know of Heaven

Sugar Maple Chronicles

Casting Spells

Laced with Magic

Spun by Sorcery

Charmed: A Sugar Maple Short Story

Spells & Stitches

Enchanted – The Wedding Story

Entangled – The Homecoming

Enraptured – The Holiday Story (coming soon)

Paradise Point

Shore Lights

Chances Are

Rocky Hill Romances

Mrs. Scrooge

Bundle of Joy

The Year the Cat Saved Christmas

Just in Time

Annie's Gift

The Rocky Hill Holiday Collection: Two novels and two novellas

About the Author

Barbara Bretton is the USA Today bestselling, award-winning author of more than 50 books. She currently has over ten million copies in print around the world. Her works have been translated into twelve languages in over twenty countries and she has received starred reviews from both *Publishers Weekly* and *Booklist*. Many of her titles are also available in audio.

Barbara has been featured in articles in *The New York Times, USA Today, Wall Street Journal, Romantic Times, Cleveland Plain Dealer, Herald News, Home News, Somerset Gazette*, among others, and has been interviewed by Independent Network News Television, appeared on the Susan Stamberg Show on NPR, and been featured in an interview with Charles Osgood of WCBS, among others.

Her awards include both Reviewer's Choice and Career Achievement Awards from Romantic Times; a RITA nomination from RWA, Gold and Silver certificates from Affaire de Coeur; the RWA Region 1 Golden Leaf; and several sales awards from Bookrak. Ms. Bretton was included in a recent edition of Contemporary Authors.

When she's not writing, Barbara can be found knitting, cooking, or reading.

She lives in New Jersey with her husband and a houseful of pets.

To subscribe to Barbara's infrequent newsletter, click here.

facebook.com/BarbaraBretton

twitter.com/BarbaraBretton

instagram.com/BarbaraBretton

youtube.com/wickedsplitty

pinterest.com/BarbaraBretton

goodreads.com/Barbara_Bretton

Excerpt from Casting Spells

In case you're new to Sugar Maple and would like to catch up with all that went before, here's a look at the first of the first book in the series, *Casting Spells.*

CHLOE
Sugar Maple, Vermont

Do you ever wonder why things happen the way they do? All of those seemingly random decisions we make throughout our lives that turn out to be not so random after all. Maybe if I had closed the shop twenty minutes earlier that night or gone for a quick walk around Snow Lake, she might still be alive today.

But I didn't and that choice changed our lives forever.

At the moment when it all began, I was down on my knees, muttering ancient curses under my breath as I tugged, pulled, and tried to convince five feet of knitted lace that it would be much happier stretched out to six plus.

If there were any magic spells out there to help a girl block a shawl I hadn't found them, and believe me, I'd looked. Blocking, like life, was equal parts intuition, brute strength, and dumb luck.

(Just in case you were wondering, I usually don't mention the dumb luck part when I give a workshop.)

That Monday night I was two hours into Blocking 101, teaching my favorite techniques to three yarn-crawling sisters from Pennsylvania, a teacher from New Jersey, and a retired rocket scientist from Florida. We had been expecting a busload of fiber fanatics from northern Maine, but a wicked early winter blizzard had stopped them somewhere west of Bangor. Two of my best friends from town, admitted knit shop groupies and world-class gossips, rounded out the class.

By the way, I'm Chloe Hobbs, owner of Sticks & Strings, voted the number one knit shop in New England two years running. I don't know exactly who did the voting, but I owe each of those wonderful knitters some quiviut and a margarita. Blog posts about the magical store in northern Vermont where your yarn never tangles, your sleeves always come out the same length, and you always, always get gauge were popping up on a daily basis, raising both my profile and my bottom line.

Sometimes I worried that this sudden, unexpected burst of fame and fortune had extended the tourist season beyond the town's comfort zone. Hiding in plain sight was harder than it sounded, but for now our secret was still safe.

A blocking board was spread open on the floor. A dark blue Spatterware bowl of T-pins rested next to it. My trusty spray bottle of warm water had been refilled twice. I probably looked like a train wreck as I crawled my way around the perimeter, pinning each scallop and point into position, but those were the breaks.

Since blocking lace was pretty much my only cardio these days, when the wolf whistle sailed overhead, I didn't bother to look up.

"Wow!" Janice Meany, owner of Cut & Curl across the street, murmured. "Those can't be real."

If I'd had any doubt about the wolf whistles, Janice's statement erased it. Last I heard, not too many women were ordering 34As from their neighborhood cosmetic surgeon.

"Implants," Lynette Pendragon declared in a voice that could be heard in the upper balcony of her family's Sugar Maple Arts Playhouse. "Or a really good wizard."

It was times like this when I wished I had inherited a tiny bit of magick from my mother. Just enough to render my indiscreet friend speechless for a second or two. Everyone in Sugar Maple knows we don't talk about wizards in front of civilians unless the conversation includes Munchkins and Oz.

Fortunately our guests had other things on their minds. "I'm glad my Howie isn't here," one of the Pennsylvania sisters breathed. "She looks like Sharon Stone. Howie has a thing for Sharon Stone."

"Sharon Stone fifteen years ago on a good day," the New Jersey schoolteacher added. "A very good day."

What can I say? I'm only a human. (And a nosy one at that.) I dumped the lace and glanced toward the front window.

Winter comes early to our part of Vermont. By the time the last of the leaf-peepers have headed down to the lesser glories of New York and Connecticut, we're digging out our snowshoes and making sure our woodpiles are well stocked. In mid-December it's dark and seriously cold by four thirty, and only the most intrepid window-shopping tourist would

ever consider strolling down Main Street without at least five layers of clothing.

The woman peering in at us was blond, tall, and around my age, but that was where the resemblance ended. I'm the kind of woman who could disappear into a crowd even if her hair was on fire. Our window shopper couldn't disappear if she tried. Her movie-star-perfect face was pressed up against the frosty glass and we had a full-frontal glimpse of bare arms, bare shoulders, and cleavage that would send Pamela Anderson running back to her surgeon.

"Am I nuts or is she naked?" I asked no one in particular.

"I think she's strapless," Janice said, but she didn't sound convinced.

"It can't be more than ten degrees out there," one of the Pennsylvanians said, exchanging looks with her sisters. "She must be crazy."

"Or drunk," Lynette offered.

"I'll bet she was mugged," the rocket scientist volunteered. "I saw a weird-looking guy lurking down the block when I parked my car."

I was tempted to tell her that the weird-looking guy was a half-asleep vampire named Buster on an ice cream run for his pregnant wife, but I figured that might not be good for business.

The possibly naked woman at the window tapped twice, mimed a shiver, then pointed toward the locked door, where the CLOSED sign was prominently displayed.

"Are you going to make her stand out there all night?" Janice asked. "Maybe she needs help."

She definitely isn't here for a new set of double points, I thought as I flipped the lock. Not that I profile my customers or anything, but I'd bet my favorite rosewoods that she had never cast on a stitch in her life and intended to keep it that way.

My second thought as she swirled past me into the shop was, Wow, she really is naked. It took a full second for me to realize that was an illusion created by a truly gifted dressmaker with access to spectacular yard goods.

My third thought--well, I didn't actually have a third thought. I was still working on the second one when she smiled at me and somewhere out there a dentist counted his T-bills.

"I'm Chloe," I said as I looked into her sea green eyes. Eyes like that usually came with magical powers (and more than a little bit of family history), but she had the vibe of the pure human about her. "I own the shop."

"Suzanne Marsden." She extended a perfectly manicured hand and I thought I caught a shiver of Scotch on her breath. "I think you might have saved my life."

"Literally or figuratively?" I asked.

I've dealt with lots of life-or-death emergencies at Sticks & Strings, but most of them included dropped stitches and too many margaritas at our Wednesday Night Knit-Ins.

She laughed as Janice and Lynette exchanged meaningful looks I tried very hard to ignore.

"I can't believe they wouldn't seat me early at the Inn. I thought

I could flirt with the bartender until my boyfriend arrived but no such luck."

It was probably the first time anyone had ever refused her anything, and she looked puzzled and annoyed in an amused kind of way.

"The Weavers can be a tad rigid," I said, studiously avoiding eye contact with my townie friends, who knew exactly why the Weavers acted the way they did. "I promise you the food's worth the aggravation."

"I left my coat in the car so I could make a big sweeping Hollywood entrance, and now I not only can't get into the damn restaurant, I locked myself out of my car and would probably have frozen to death out there if you hadn't taken pity on me and opened your door."

"Honey, you're in Vermont," Janice said. "You can't go around like that up here. You'll freeze your nipples off."

"She said she has a coat," I reminded Janice a tad sharply. As a general rule I find it best not to discuss politics, religion, or my customer's nipples in the shop. "It's locked in her car."

"With my cell and my skis and my ice skates," Suzanne said with a theatrical eye roll. "All I need is to use your phone so I can call Triple A."

"Oh, don't bother with them," Lynette said with a wave of her hand. "They'll take all night to get up here. My daughter Vonnie can have it open in a heartbeat."

Suzanne's perfectly groomed right eyebrow rose slightly. "If it's not too much trouble, that would be great."

Clearly she thought Vonnie was majoring in grand theft auto at Sugar Maple High, but that was a whole lot better than telling her that the teenager could make garage doors roll open three towns away just by thinking about them.

There were some things tourists were better off not knowing.

I shot Lynette a look. "So you're going to go call Vonnie now, right?"

We both knew she had already put out the call to her daughter, but we're all about keeping up appearances here in Sugar Maple.

155

"I'm on it," Lynette said and went off in search of her cell phone.

I turned back to our visitor, who was up to her elbows in a basket of angora roving waiting to be spun into yarn, while Penelope, the ancient store cat who shared the basket, ignored her.

"This is glorious. I've thought about learning to knit but--" She shrugged. "You know how it is."

Well, not really. I've been knitting since I was old enough to hold a pair of needles.

"I'll be spinning that next week," I told her while we waited for Lynette to return, "then knitting it up into a shawl."

She wandered to the stack of shawls on the shelf and fingered a kid silk Orenburg I had on display. "Don't tell me you made this?"

"Chloe knitted everything in the shop," Janice volunteered.

"Impossible!" Suzanne Marsden looked over at me. "Did you really? I love handmade garments and this is heirloom quality."

She might have been lying through her porcelain veneers but it was all the encouragement I needed. I whipped out the Orenburg and was treated to the kind of adulation usually reserved for rock stars.

"Amazing," Suzanne breathed as I laid the shawl across her slender shoulders. "You couldn't possibly have made this without divine intervention."

I started to spout my usual it's-all-just-knit-and-purl shop owner spiel when to my surprise the truth popped out instead. "It almost put me into intensive care," I admitted to the background laughter of my friends, "but I made it to the other side."

And then I showed her the trick that either sent prospective knitters running back to their crochet hooks or won them over forever. I slipped my mother's wedding band off my right forefinger and passed the shawl through the small circle of Welsh gold.

"How much?" Suzanne asked.

"It's not for sale," Lynette answered before I had the chance to open my mouth. "Chloe never sells her Orenburgs."

"In my experience there are exceptions to every absolute."

Suzanne favored me with a smile that was a half-degree away from flirtatious. "Name your price."

"Dangerous words to use in front of a shop owner," I said lightly, "but Lynette is right. The shawls on that shelf are for display only."

Suzanne met my eyes, and I saw something behind the smile that took me by surprise.

Pretty people aren't supposed to be sad. Isn't that the story you were told when you were a little girl? Pretty people are supposed to get a free ride through this life and possibly the next one too.

That was the thing about running a shop. Every now and then a customer managed to push the right buttons and my business sense, shaky at the best of times, went up in smoke.

I swiped her platinum AmEx through the machine and slid the receipt across the counter for her signature.

"Would you like me to wrap it for you?" I asked while Lynette and Janice kept the other customers amused.

"No, thanks," she said, pirouetting in front of the cheval mirror in the corner. "I'll wear it."

Lynette popped back in. "Vonnie texted me," she said to Suzanne. "Your car's unlocked and the Inn is open for business."

Suzanne flashed us a conspiratorial grin. "My boyfriend always keeps me waiting. It wouldn't hurt him to do a little waiting himself."

But she didn't keep him waiting long. She signed her receipt, made a few polite noises, then hurried back out into the darkness.

"I'd give anything to see the boyfriend," one of the Pennsylvania sisters said after the door clicked shut behind Suzanne Marsden. "I'll bet we're talking major hottie."

"Johnny Depp hot or George Clooney hot?" the schoolteacher from New Jersey asked, and everyone laughed.

The rocket scientist gave out a cross between a snicker and a snort. "That woman has future trophy wife written all over her. Odds are he's old, wrinkled, and rich."

"Maybe she loves him," I said then immediately wished I'd kept my big mouth shut.

Janice and Lynette exchanged glances and I didn't need extrasensory powers to know exactly what they were thinking. I shot them my best "don't you dare" warning look. One thing I didn't need was another lecture on love from Sugar Maple's two most dangerous matchmakers.

Blocking lace seemed a little anticlimactic to me after Suzanne's mini-drama. I was seriously tempted to excuse myself for a minute then race up the street so I could peek through the front window of the Inn and eyeball the guy she was meeting, but that wasn't how Sticks & Strings had maintained its ranking as the number one knit shop in New England two years running.

So I stayed put, but that didn't mean I was happy about it.

It was a little before ten by the time everyone exchanged names and phone numbers and e-mail addresses. I handed out goodie bags of knitting gadgets and yarn samples and smiled at the oohs and ahhs of appreciation. Welcome to the dark side, ladies. Before long they would need an extra room to house their stash.

I let out a loud sigh of relief as I sank into one of the over-stuffed chairs near the Ashford wheels. "I actually broke into a sweat blocking that shawl." I flapped the hem of my T-shirt for emphasis.

Janice rolled her eyes. "You're not going to get any sympathy from me. Try giving a full body wax to an overweight eighty-five-year-old man with more wrinkles than a shar-pei. Now that's a workout."

Too much information. What went on behind the closed doors of Cut & Curl was none of my business.

"Seriously. I thought that shawl was going to get the better of me."

"Our visitor is the one who got the better of you," Lynette said. "You barely recouped the cost of the yarn."

Lynette was always trying to give me business advice, and I was always doing my best to ignore her. "I thought we had a great group tonight. Definitely better than the carload of mystery writers who drove in for the finishing workshop last month. Now that was a big mistake."

Leave it to mystery writers to wonder why the Inn flashed a NO OCCUPANCY sign but didn't have any visitors.

"I'm talking about the shawl. She practically stole it from you." Lynette could be like a dog with a stack of short ribs.

"Don't exaggerate."

"You must have spent twice that on yarn."

"I didn't spend anything. That was hand-spun from my mother's stash." When my mother died, one of the things she left me was a basket of roving that remained full to overflowing no matter how many hours I spent at my wheel, and another was a love of all things fiber.

"Good gods," Lynette shrieked. "It's worse than I thought."

"I'm not crazy," I said, slightly annoyed. "Lilith checks the roving twice a year to make sure it's free from any traveling spells."

Lynette was mollified, but just barely. "You really should drive down to Brattleboro and take a class in small business management," she went on. "Cyrus said it's the best money we ever spent."

Lynette and Cyrus were owners/operators of the Sugar Maple Arts Playhouse at the corner of Carrier Court and Willard Grove. Cyrus was one of the SMAP's favorite performers, which, considering the fact that he was a shapeshifter, made casting a snap. Lynette and their daughters Vonnie and Iphigenia were also shapeshifters and had been known to round out Cyrus's repertory company on more than one occasion. Their sons, the unfortunately named Gilbert and Sullivan were occasionally pressed into service too, but Gil and Sully were quickly reaching the age where it would take cash to turn them into orphaned pirates.

"So you'll think about it?" Lynette pressed. "If you sign up before the end of the year, Cyrus gets a fifty-dollar rebate."

"I'll think about it," I said, "but it's pretty hard to get away these days."

"You don't want to get away," Janice said as she rinsed out the teapot.

"That's right," Lynette observed as she swept crumbs off the worktable and tossed them into the trash. "You're all about the work lately."

"It would do you good to take a little trip." Janice reached for the coffeepot. "I can't remember the last time you went away for a night or two."

"I can," Lynette said as she fluffed up the pillows on the leather sofa near the fireplace. "It was when she was seeing that lawyer from New Hampshire."

Janice frowned. "That has to be--what? Four, five years ago?"

"Almost six," I said, "and I don't want to talk about it."

"You can't possibly still blame us for that."

"Putting a spell on our car wasn't very funny. We could have frozen to death up there in the woods."

"We moved the relationship along," Lynette broke in. "You should be grateful."

"Lynnie's right," Janice said. "We saved you from making a terrible mistake."

"Howard was handsome, smart, and independently wealthy. Where's the mistake in that?"

"He was human," Janice said. "It wouldn't have worked."

"I'm human," I reminded her.

"Only half," Lynette said. "Your mother was a sorceress."

"Yes, she was, but we all know I take after my father." I had his height, his hair, and his humanness. There wasn't the slightest bit of magick about me and there never had been. I couldn't see into the future or shapeshift or bend spoons with the power of my mind. I was as solid and earthbound as one of the maple trees in Willard Grove.

"Nothing good happens when magick meets human," Janice went on. "Don't tempt fate, honey. Stick with your own kind."

What they meant was, "Your mother fell in love with a human and see what happened to her."

I was six years old when my parents died in a car crash not far from the Toothaker Bridge. The car skidded on black ice and slammed into a towering maple tree. My human father had been killed instantly. My sorceress mother lingered for two days while Sorcha and Lilith and all the people who loved her did everything in their power to convince her to stay, but in the end Guinevere chose to leave this world to be with the only man she would ever love.

My memories of that time were all in soft focus. Mostly I remember Sorcha, who had opened up her life and her home to me and made me her own.

Sometimes I hated my mother for making that choice. What kind of woman would choose to leave her daughter alone in the world? Depending on the time of day and how much wine I'd consumed, I either found her decision achingly romantic or the act of a supremely selfish woman.

"You're not listening," I said to my friends. "I don't have magick and I probably never will."

"You never know what might happen," Janice said. "You always were a late bloomer. You were the last in your class to start wearing a bra."

I was also the last in my class to score a date to the senior prom, something that still stings even now, thirteen years later. If it hadn't been for my pal Gunnar, I wouldn't have gone at all. "And your point is?"

Lynette leaned forward, all dark-eyed intensity. "My mother told me that your mother didn't come into her full powers until she fell in love."

"But she had some powers before she met my father," I reminded my friends. "I remember the stories. Why can't you both accept the fact that I'm never going to be more than I am right now?"

They exchanged another one of those knowing glances that reminded me of the housewives of Wisteria Lane.

"No matchmaking," I said, barely stifling a yawn. "Absolutely, positively not. I am way too old for matchmaking." Okay, so I was only thirty, but blind dates aged a girl in dog years.

"But he's perfect for you."

"That's what you said about the last one."

Janice had the decency to look a tiny bit sheepish. "I'll admit Jacob was a mistake."

"Jacob was a troll."

Literally.

"Midge Stallworth forgot to mention that. We thought he was vampire like the rest of the family."

"If the Universe wants me to find someone, they'll send me a hot alpaca farmer who likes to spin."

"Honey, you know we're only thinking about your happiness." Lynette patted my hand.

Maybe they were thinking about my happiness, but they were also thinking about the accident just before Christmas last year. A bus carrying a high school hockey team en route to Brattleboro blew a tire and careened down an embankment near the Sugar Maple town limits, killing the goalie and the coach.

Things like that weren't supposed to happen here. Accidents, crime, illness, all the things that plagued every other town in America, didn't happen here. Or at least they hadn't up until recently.

Over three hundred years ago one of my sorcerer ancestors cast a protective charm over the town designed to shield Sugar Maple from harm for as long as one of her line walked the earth and--well, you guessed it. I'm the last descendant of Aerynn, and if you thought your family was on your case to marry and produce offspring, try having an entire town mixing potions, casting runes, and weaving spells designed to hook you up with Mr. Right.

"The accident was random chance," I said, trying to ignore the chill racing up my spine as I remembered the crowd of reporters who had flooded the area. "The weather was terrible. It could have happened anywhere."

"But it didn't happen anywhere," Janice said. "It happened here and it shouldn't have."

"Jan's right," Lynette said. "The spell is growing weaker with every year that passes. I can feel the difference."

Janice nodded. "We all do."

I didn't but that was no surprise. I could only take them at their word on this, same as I did on everything else I couldn't see or hear or understand.

"Cyrus met a charming selkie named Glenn at the Scottish Faire last week," Lynette went on.

"She already dated a selkie," Janice reminded her. "It wasn't a good match."

"I dated a selkie?" The parade of recent losers had mercifully blurred in my memory.

"You said his breath smelled like smoked salmon."

I shuddered. "I'll skip the selkies, thanks."

"You get used to it," Janice, who was married to a selkie, said. "Truth is, you'd skip them all if we let you."

She was right about that.

"Just keep Saturday nights open," Lynette said. "That's all I'm asking."

As far as I could tell, my Saturday nights were open from now until the next millennium. I nodded and stifled another yawn. "No trolls, no selkies," I said. "And he has to be at least six feet tall before the magic kicks in."

"Not a problem," Janice said. "Tall is good."

"Human might be nice for a change."

They looked at me, then at each other, and burst into raucous laughter.

"Honey," Lynette said as she patted my arm, "around here human might not be your best choice."

I wasn't usually prickly about their wariness about humans, but that night it got under my skin. It wasn't like I actually thought Mr. Right was going to show up at Sticks & Strings one snowy winter day searching for the perfect ski sweater to wear on the slopes. But I did think love was possible. It had happened for my parents, hadn't it? Maybe they hadn't managed the happy ending part of the equation, but for a little while I saw what real magic was all about and I didn't want to settle for anything less.

Now you know why I had five cats, one TiVo, and a stash of yarn I couldn't knit my way through in six lifetimes.

I mean, what were the odds that the perfect man would not only show up in Sugar Maple, but also be okay with the fact that the town wasn't the picture-postcard New England town our Chamber of Commerce would have you believe, but a village of vampires, werewolves, elves, faeries, and everything else your parents told you didn't really exist?

Or that he would be okay with the fact that the woman he wanted to spend his life with had a few surprises lurking in her own gene pool?

Ten million to one sounded about right to me.

Besides, Sugar Maple was doing fine without my help. We had a thriving tourist trade and zero crime. What other town could make that claim? It seemed to me that Aerynn's protective blessing was still getting the job done even if we had had a few close calls over the last year or two.

The blessing's strength might be weakening, but we still had time to figure this out before it vanished altogether. All we needed was a frothy little protective charm to cover us until I either found the man of my dreams or came up with a Plan B.

And maybe things would have worked out that way if, just a few hours after she left my shop, Suzanne Marsden hadn't been murdered.

End of Chapter 1

CPSIA information can be obtained
at www.ICGtesting.com
Printed in the USA
LVHW090529141118
597094LV00002B/535/P